CRAIG HALLORAN

ZOMBIE REHAB

BEWARE OF ZOMBIES

BOOK 2

CONTENTS

Zombie Rehab: Impact Series: Book 2

Copyright August 2012 by Craig Halloran

TWO-TEN BOOK PRESS

P.O. Box 4215, Charleston, WV 25364

Amazon Edition

ISBN Paperback: 978-0-9884642-1-6

ISBN Ebook: 978-0-9884642-0-9

Information about this author and his other works available at:

WWW.CRAIGHALLORAN.COM

Publisher's Note:

This book is a work of fiction. Names, characters, places, and incidents either are the product of the author's imagination or are used fictitiously, and any resemblance to actual persons, living or dead, events, or locales is entirely coincidental.

❀ Created with Vellum

1

LOCATION UNKNOWN

Location Unknown

He was moving under a series of bright fluorescent lights. The glare hurt his eyes, but he was determined to keep them open. He had to figure out where he was. His mind fought to regain control of his body, which strained against the leather bonds that had him strapped to the gurney. At least, he thought he was fighting, but his limbs were more like jelly, and his mind was mush. The only thing he recognized was the thump-thump of the gurney wheels rolling over the tiles of the long corridor.

He could have sworn he was hung over and being pushed in a grocery cart over an unpaved parking lot. He retched. His mouth filled with the tang of bile. A blurry figure jerked his head up and was shouting something unintelligible. He was dizzy; the lights above were beginning to blur together like the white dashes on a highway. A sharp pain pierced his arm, causing him to break out into a cold sweat. *What is going on?*

There were several of them, shaped like men but moving like ghosts. He tried to find an outline, recognize a face, let his mind find something that was familiar. Instead, there was nothing, just a corridor that began to swirl and spin into a vortex. He felt euphoria as his frantic eyelids became heavy and he plunged into the darkness.

His eyes snapped open. Something was chiseling on his face. His body convulsed and shuddered as a group of faceless people scrambled and screamed.

"He's resisting! He's resisting! Dammit, who prepped him! Get the anesthesiologist."

Bloodied gloves were holding sharp shining objects, and the ghosts began to rush around him. A pair of eyes looked deep into his, large and disturbing.

"Give him more! Give him more ..."

He faded into a bright patch of lilies.

HE WOKE up incapacitated and in pain. His eyes flickered open only to gaze at the darkness of a quiet room. There was a smell of chlorine and ammonia in the air, and urine, too. Inside his sluggish mind he sensed someone else in the room, at his side, gazing with heavy eyes.

"Mrmphh ..." he moaned.

He regretted it. His jaw felt like it was broken, and the rest of his face seemed like a busted vase. *Ah ... I don't understand! Help me someone! Help me!*

A shadow was moving by his side, silent. Perfume. It was nice, like something from heaven. A figure crossed in front of him, this shape more defined than the last, comely, tangible, real. *No, don't leave me!* The figure passed into a dark frame and vanished. His eyes began to water. He wanted to move his arms and legs, but he couldn't feel them. He began to wonder if he even had them. Something soft was obstructing part of his view, like cotton, tape, or gauze. *Hospital? Hospital!*

He tried to remember the last thing that happened to him. His mind was so dreary, exhausted like a car that had run out of gas. Nothing seemed capable of unlocking the vault of knowledge that was within him. It was blocked, either by his own desire or something else. He knew he should be able to remember something, but he couldn't.

There were sounds now. He could hear the hum of an air conditioner and feel the cool air rushing on his eyes.

Beep..Beep..Beep.

It was a steady sound that he found comforting. He was somewhere, and he was alive. That had to be a good thing. He just wished his face didn't hurt so much. What had happened to him? Where in the world was he? As he stared up at the ceiling, he noticed the tiles were loose and water stained, and there was a drip coming from somewhere, landing on the floor and not in a sink. He began to wonder how it was he could understand what these things were but he couldn't remember a thing about who he was. Everything was confusing.

"Mrmphh! MRMRPHH!"

Pain exploded in his face, and the beeping at his bedside began to increase its pace. Two figures in light green scrubs rushed upon him from the darkened doorway. One was a man and the other a woman, he could tell that much, but they were both faceless. As he turned his neck to get a better look it felt like someone was driving a stake in his neck.

"Hrrumph!" he tried to say help.

Tears were filling his eyes as his mind pleaded for them to say something to him ... anything. He felt a delicate hand dabbing the water from his eyes with a soft towel. He felt like his heart was going to burst, the feeling of humanity so close to touching him. He just wanted to reconnect, try to find out if he was still a human. *Why can't I feel my limbs? Why?* He felt the hand pulling away, and he let out an audible sob. *NO! Come back!*

He could make out the pair, huddled at the end of the bed. The man towered over the woman, and even though he was whispering, his voice was as deep as a well and callous as a stone.

"Do not let him revive again, you idiot."

"I'm sorry, Doctor," she said with a quiver in her voice, "I swear I haven't missed a single dose. Not one, and I've checked the other shifts, too."

"Shut up, I don't need your feeble explanation. Give me his chart!"

As he lay in the bed he could see the doctor scribbling something on the clipboard. Then the big man shoved the clipboard into her hand and said, "That dose should take care of it, for another month at least."

What! Another month! I've been under for a month? No. That can't be!

He swore he could feel the bones in his face seeping into his brain, and even though he couldn't remember anything, he could recall despair. Something deep down inside him triggered a small chip of memories, horrible ones, something that had just happened that he'd just as soon forget. The doctor's unpleasant tone interrupted his thoughts.

"Nurse, I don't want to have to remind you that if you screw this up again ... I'll be getting rid of you. And you know what that means, don't you?"

He could hear her sobbing reply, "Y-yes sir, I m mean Doctor Zhan—"

Slap!

He could feel his own cheek stinging from the blow as the nurse crumpled to the ground.

Hey! Why'd you hit her for?

"Mrmmf Fumphnhr!" It hurt so bad to say it he almost blacked out, and his stomach began to churn. He could hear the man walking away on heavy footsteps as the woman struggled to rise from the ground. He watched as her fuzzy outline slowly stepped behind him. He heard the sound of a small plastic wheel grinding and then something ice cold ran in his veins.

"NO!"

The pain was so bad, but he would rather deal with that than be knocked out for another month. Then he saw her face before his: round, sweet, and black. She was whispering something in his ear.

"It's gonna be okay, Honey. It's going to be okay, just hang in there."

Please tell me where I am?

As the pain began to subside, he felt something warm squeezing his hand. It was her hand in his, and it felt wonderful as he drifted away into a dreamless slumber.

2

WASHINGTON, DC

TWO SUITED MEN WERE SEATED ON A PARK BENCH NEAR the Jefferson Memorial, soaking in the sun of a cool fall day. The leaves were turning in some places, but most of them still maintained their rich green colors. Both men sat comfortably, talking back and forth and nodding. The humming of a black Cadillac engine sounded nearby, with one stout man in a navy blue suit sitting on the hood and smoking. A semi-automatic pistol could be seen strapped inside is jacket, but none of the passersby noticed. He seemed to be enjoying the fresh air almost as much as his cigarette. He let out a breath of smoke, flicked his ashes, then took another puff. If he had any interest in what the men were saying, he didn't show it. Instead, he watched and waited.

The taller man, bearded in white, turned, rested his elbow on the back of the bench, and faced the other. The younger man, maybe forty, remained seated with his hands clasped, stooped over with his elbows resting on his knees, eyes gazing at the tip of the Washington Monument in the distance.

"Come on, Jack, it's going to be fine. She'll come back to her senses. She needs you, and she loves you," the older man said in a rich and soothing voice.

Jack shook his head as he ran his fingers back through his thick brown hair. He opened his mouth to speak, but no words came. The older man squeezed his shoulder with a reassuring grip and patted him on the back.

"Jack, women do crazy things. Even before the zombies they were crazy. It's just stress, that's all. Some time at home with her mother will do her some good. I know her mom; she'll talk some sense into her."

Jack took a deep breath as he sat up and then leaned back against the bench. "Her mom seems to be just as testy these days. I keep calling Angie there, but her mom's been pretty nasty. Called me a selfish bastard."

"Geez, Becky said that? That doesn't seem like her at all. She was always so sweet. Hey, let me give Becky a call; I think I can smooth things over."

"Don, I appreciate it, but right now I get the feeling that any more attempted interventions will make them madder."

"Hah ... Jack, they love getting mad. I'd keep it up

because you know what will happen if you leave Angie alone too long?"

"What?"

"She'll get even madder," Don said, smiling and patting him on the shoulder.

"Great."

Reaching over, Don grabbed his custom computer and set it on his lap. His aged fingers were as quick as a teen's as he loaded one screen after the other. Whatever he was doing, Jack wasn't paying much attention.

Don's voice took on a dire tone as he asked, "You haven't let Angie in on anything that's going on, have you?"

Jack stiffened.

"No, absolutely not. I swear. That's the problem, Don, we're close, and I'm keeping in all of these secrets."

"Is she still prying into your business?"

"No ... Yes, it depends on the mood she's in, I guess."

"Listen to me, Jack: you can't ever—I mean ever—tell her a thing, or it's over. The WHS has trusted you with a great deal, and if you blow it you'll be deader than a zombie before dawn."

Jack sagged in his chair saying, "I know."

"Angie and Becky will be, too." Don cleared his throat. "I'm sorry, I mean, you're just out of their program, a couple of years, but still new, and you somehow wound up with knowledge you didn't even know existed. But that knowledge gives you power, Jack. It protects you and your family. It protects me, your uncle, and you have to trust me and believe me that you cannot share what you know with anyone. Got it, Jack?"

Jack patted his uncle on his knee and said, "I won't let you down, Don. I haven't said a word, and I won't. Not ever. You know you don't have to worry about that. My mind is like a bank vault; even the most brilliant thieves would have trouble getting in there."

Don laughed and said, "Okay, I know. I just want you to be careful. Extra careful. But you've got to get your household back to normal, else it will arouse suspicion. I figure your mother in-law's house is already bugged."

"Damn. You really think so?"

"Just being a little paranoid for you. Look, you're gonna have to give Angie a convincing lie to get her back home. You're going to have to convince her you were hiding something believable. Tell her you had an after hours encounter with a cocktail waitress or something."

"What? She'll castrate me!"

"Just a close call, nothing overly intimate. It'll work. I mean, you're a good-looking guy. It's not like another woman hitting on you should surprise her."

"Great," Jack sighed, "and if that doesn't work?"

"Then flip it on her, and accuse her of hiding something like an affair. Check her texts and Facebook posts. I'm sure there are plenty of saps out there flirting with her. Use it against her."

"Gee Uncle Don, you sure are cold."

"No, I'm a survivor, a realist. The walls of this world are closing in on us. The waters are rising fast; I'm just trying to keep my head above water. Yours as well. Now, let's get down to business. What's the latest on the XT Formula?"

3

INSTITUTE, WEST VIRGINIA

"HENRY? HENRY BAWKULA, IS THAT YOU?"

He tried to look away, get into his car and go, but it was too late. She had caught him, and a discomforting feeling churned in his stomach. Still, he pulled his ball cap farther down on his head and hung the gasoline hose back on the pump.

He pressed the "NO" button that was asking him if he wanted a receipt, and when he turned he was face-to-face with Jennifer.

"Henry, seriously, I know you weren't about to blow me off. It's been almost ten years, and I can't believe I'm seeing you again. I'm ... I'm so happy," she said, wrapping her arms around him and giving him a big hug. He tried to pull away, but she was unwilling to let him go. He wasn't so sure he wanted her to let go, either, as there had been a time, not so long ago, when she had been the most normal thing in his life. And there she was, as pretty as she could be.

Jennifer, it's great to see you," he said, managing to break her embrace. "I-I didn't know if you were still around. I mean, I'm sorry to put it that way." He shook his head. "It's just that, well with the apocalypse and all I wasn't sure if ... if—"

She put her finger on his lips.

"Shhh Henry, I'm okay. You don't have to worry, me and Mom and Dad and Roger are doing great. We were in Arizona when all of that happened. We were some of the lucky ones."

Just cut it short; you have to go. "I'm glad to hear it. We uh ... well, weren't so fortunate. Look, I have to go."

"Henry! I know you aren't just going to leave me hanging like this. So many people are gone, and now I just happen to run into my last surviving boyfriend, and you want to run off on me? No, Sir. We have some catching up to do."

Jennifer sounded convincing enough. She always had been forward, driven, and desirable. All he had ever wanted to do was please her back then, but that was high school, and the world had changed an awful lot since then.

"I'm sorry, Jennifer, but I can't. Just give me your number and I'll call you, I promise," he said, forcing himself between her and his back bumper.

She pinned him against the car with her body and kissed him. *Oh no. This can't be happening.* But it was happening; a flood of passion began to consume them both underneath the roof of the Go-Mart parking lot. He shoved her away.

"Are you crazy, Jennifer? I'm not alone here. I've got to go. You have to understand that. Just give me your—"

But it was too late. He was caught. She was caught, and the storm was coming. Henry took one last look at Jennifer, noting her sweet smile, silky black hair, bejeweled eyes over top of a rich and bewitching figure.

"What is it, Henry? You look like you just saw a zombie."

He swallowed hard and said, "No, worse, sort of. You're about to meet my girlfriend. My very jealous girlfriend."

Jennifer turned around in time to catch Tori's last few bouncing steps. Henry swore he heard thunder overhead as his butt remained seated on the bumper of his car. Tori's twelve pack of beer bottles rattled as she extended her hand toward Jennifer.

"Hi, I'm Tori ... Henry's girlfriend. And who might you be?"

"Oh, I'm so sorry. I'm Jennifer, Henry's ex-girlfriend."

What? Oh geez! "Uh, that was a long time ago, over a decade."

Tori still held her hand out and slowly Jennifer extended hers as she said, "Well, it seems we both have great taste in brilliant men. It's so nice to meet you—"

Jennifer's eyes glanced down at their shaking hands. Henry watched as her body stiffened and she tried to pull her arm away. Tori held her fast. Jennifer looked over her shoulder at him, eyes pleading for mercy.

"Tori, let go," he said, rising up from the bumper.

Jennifer's knees began to buckle.

"LET GO, TORI!"

Jennifer gasped as she tore her arm away. Without looking back, she jumped into her car, tore out of the parking lot, and didn't wave good-bye. Tori did, however, waving her gnarled half-dead arm like a banner from the 4th of July.

"Tori, put your arm down and get in the car. Now!"

They both slammed their doors as they got in. Henry had the car in drive and had punched it to the floor before she even got her seat-belt buckled.

"Way to go, Tori!"

"What? You can't be mad at me. You're the one sucking face with some woman in the parking lot!"

"I'm sorry—look, I'm sorry. She took me by surprise. I tried to get away, she just—"

Tori laughed, "She just what, over powered you? Give me a break, you cheater!"

"What? I'm not a cheater! You know better than that. Now get a hold of yourself."

Tori didn't say a word; she just stared out of her

side window and brushed her hair back from her face with her odd hand.

All Henry could think about was getting back to the complex so he could bury himself back in his work, and Tori would do the same. There had been other highs and lows between them since they departed the Zombie Day Care under the most bizarre circumstances. Normal was no longer an option in his life. Embracing the abnormal to survive was his only option.

"You're sick of being with me, aren't you? Now that I'm deformed and all, you are wanting something better, perfect, like I used to be until you drug me into that day care."

"Don't go down this road, Tori. You said you wouldn't bring it up anymore. I told you to stay outside, but you wouldn't listen. Can't you just be thankful that you're alive?"

"I'm a freak!" she said, slamming her gnarled hand into the dashboard.

"Hey-Hey! Don't do that. Quit acting like a child. You're still beautiful; you know that."

It was true. Tori was every bit as sexy as she ever was. Her auburn hair was lustrous, her buxom figure not as soft as before, but firm. Still, her sweet face was drained, almost haggard some days, but nobody paid her hand any mind as they were too busy looking at the rest of her. As strange as her hand was, it wasn't nearly as bad as she made it out to be.

He glanced over at the appendage, but Tori tucked it under her leg and glared. From the elbow down you could see the flesh was pasty and gray. The fingers remained stiff and bent, the nails dead and black. Henry figured she could have coped with it better if it was her own arm to begin with, but it wasn't. It was someone else's, thicker and stronger like a man's, but they were assured it was a woman's. A woman lumberjack maybe. Henry always wondered about that. At least it worked, and it was better than nothing there at all.

Tori tore open the twelve pack of beer and pulled out a bottle.

"What are you doing now?"

"I'm having a beer," she said, turning the top off of one and tilting it to her lips.

"Tori, quit that. Now you're just being silly. You don't even drink."

"Well, today I'm starting a new diet."

Henry reached and grabbed the bottle saying, "Gimme that."

"Oh Henry, don't take my bottle. Please Henry don't." She said it like she was on a vaudeville stage, exasperated and silly.

Henry tugged at the bottle that was in the vise-like grip of her replaced hand. She was giggling at his futile efforts.

"What's the matter, Henry, can't the big boy take the bottle from the little girl?"

The car almost crashed into the rail as Henry jerked the wheel over and weaved back and forth between the single lanes before getting the car back under control. He let go of the bottle.

"Geez, Tori! You're gonna cause a wreck. Now quit being a baby and put that beer back. It's for the party. Stupid Rudy! And we're on our way to work! Stupid complex! Stupid everything!" he shouted.

The thought of going back to the complex filled him with dread, as each passing hour approached, to the appointed time. He and Tori had been granted three weeks of leave after having been inside the dreadful complex for the prior six months. That's what the World Humanitarian Society had done: given him another job, less than thirty miles from the last one. He had tried to quit, but he wasn't given much choice. He wanted to run, but there wouldn't be any escape. They had made all of that perfectly clear in all the briefings that followed the incident at the Guthrie Facility, home of the Zombie Day Care.

He felt Tori reach out and grab his hand—with her normal one—and squeeze. She scooted closer and said, "I'm sorry, Henry, it's just that, you know it's that time—"

"I know, that time of the month."

"No, Jackhole!" she said, squeezing his hand, "It's the anniversary of the day I lost my parents, Idiot!" She let go and scooted back away.

After he pulled off the highway, the car brakes

squealed as he came to a stop. *Idiot would be correct.* Looking through the windshield, his body filled with dread. In the distance, a ten foot high limestone wall stretched over a hundred yards, with a chain-link gate in the center. He could see some of the brick-red building through the gate and some of the many tree tops that jutted over the top of the wall. He wanted to turn around.

"You ready?" he said, looking over at Tori's pouting face.

She shrugged.

"Look, I'm sorry. I didn't realize it was your parents, uh, you know. I'm sorry."

"Forget about it, Henry. Besides, it almost is that time of the month, too. But you're still gonna make things right once we get in there."

Allowing himself a faint smile, he looked over at her and said, "So you forgive me?"

"Of course. You're all I've got, Henry ... all I ever wanted. I just wish things were different. I hate being in there as much as you. But as long as I'm with you, then it doesn't really matter where I am."

He looked into her pretty eyes, held her face in his hands, and kissed her. When he finished, she opened her eyes and said, "You owe me a lot more than that, Henry. Now, let's get this over with."

He nodded his head, put the car in drive, and slowly headed down the road towards the front gate. Once again he would have to make the most of it, but he'd rather turn around. The sun was lowering in the horizon, and a flock of birds burst from the trees behind the wall. He swore he could hear something screaming. Tori grabbed his hand as his stomach began to knot. Six months. Six more months of living among the dead. The complex was a place filled with the unexpected and unnatural. *Forget everything you just left. That was normal. Check your humanity at the gate. Forget your sanity. Embrace the insanity. Think abnormal. Welcome back to the Zombie Rehab.*

4

LOCATION UNKNOWN

THE NEXT TIME he woke up, things were different. The room had changed, and he was starving. The room was illuminated by a blurry light above him, that caused his eyes to ache. He was thirsty. He tried to swallow, but his mouth was raw and sore. He shifted in his bed, and when he heard the steel framework beneath him groan, a thrill raced down his spine. *I'm moving.*

As he turned his head, he noticed a small metal dresser across the room and a heavy wooden door. When he realized he was partially sitting up, he managed to look around some more. No windows, but there was an air conditioning unit rattling along the wall, alongside a padded metal chair and a table. He reached his hand over his stomach as it groaned. *My hand, I can feel my hand!*

He held his hand up to his face and watched it tremble as he opened and closed his fingers. He couldn't feel his legs, but managed to pull his knees up into a bent position. *Thank God, I can move!* He was still weak, hungry, and confused. *What is this place?* The haziness in his mind seemed to be lifting like a fog as he peered around the little room. It looked like an old hospital room, decades old, with the original paint, trim, and checkered floors. The room was stuffy, the air from the air conditioner stale, but for some reason he was still thankful that he was breathing. He just had a hard time remembering the last thing he was doing.

He reached and grabbed a bar that was hanging from the ceiling and pulled himself up. A sharp pain stabbed his belly, and his face ached. He tried to remember if he had been in some kind of accident, then he remembered the gauze, the doctor, and the nurse. There were bandages on his face, or something like that. He rubbed his face, his eyes, nose, and head. No medical tape or gauze, just a beard. He didn't remember ever having a beard. That's when he noticed a small metal sink in the corner and pulled his legs down onto the floor. There was a mirror hanging cock-eyed over the sink, but the surface was dingy and faded. He managed to push himself up onto his feet and stand. His head swam as the floor began to wobble beneath his shaking feet, and he fell. Every bone in his body shuddered with pain as he lay on the floor trembling, tears streaming from his eyes. He wanted to cry for help, but he was too scared. That doctor was frightening. What was his name, *Zhan?*

The floor was cold, and his teeth began to chatter as he fought his way off his back and onto his elbows. His chest was heaving now, and his forehead was beaded with sweat as he shivered. That's when he saw beneath the door: shadows, silent and mysterious, passing by. He couldn't help but wonder what would happen if they came in and saw him on the floor. Would he be in trouble? Would they knock him out again and for how long? A hundred thoughts began rushing through his head as he low crawled towards the sink. His ancestral instincts were urging him on. *Must escape.* Adrenaline was fueling his strenuous effort as he managed to make it to his hands and knees. The hard tiles were painful on his knees as his elbows quaked under the strain to move forward, but he pressed on.By the time he reached the bottom of the sink, he was exhausted and wondering how he would find the energy to pull himself up. His tongue was thick in his dry mouth, and all he wanted more than anything was a drink of something wet. That's when he noticed the shadows underneath the door had stopped. The sound of muffled voices was coming from the other side. What was he going to say when they came in? *Please don't come in. Please, not yet.*

Curled up on the floor, he let his fear begin to overtake reason. He closed his eyes and waited. The sound of the muffled voices faded, and when he opened his eyes again the shadows were gone from underneath the door. Relief washed through him, but something else did as well. A sense—primitive within— had awakened. A bit of anger was rising, too, as the images of the living and the dead began to surface in his mind. *I'm alive.* He reached up and grabbed the lip of the sink, gathered his legs underneath him, and pulled himself up. *Almost there. Come on, I've gotta have more in me than this.*

He gasped and grunted, and the strength in his feeble arms and legs fought the gravity that was holding his big body down.

"No!" he gasped again as he made it up to his knees and began to slip back down. It seemed like the entire earth was against him, pulling him back down into the abyss, but he had been there before. He wasn't going back. He hung on to the sink and squatted down on his feet, then summoned everything he had as his shaking body rose to his feet. *I made it!* He wiped the sweat from his eyes and looked into the blurry mirror. He didn't recognize the man in the mirror, a greasy head of long brown hair and a scruffy beard that hid most of his face. Nothing was right. *All out of place.* His fingers brushed over his cheeks, nose, and chin. Tears formed in his eyes. *I've gone mad.* He touched the image in the mirror, then pulled his fingers back. He was changed, different, no longer who he once was. No longer the man he thought he was. But the eyes were the mirror to the soul, and those brown eyes he saw were still his own. There was no doubt in his mind that the man he was looking at was Nate McDaniel, the Man Who Saved the World. He heard footsteps and twirled around. *I've got to get out of here.*

He licked his hairy lips with his dry tongue. He felt like he could drink a river. The spigot squeaked as he turned it on and let the cold water run over his fingertips. It felt like something from heaven. He grabbed a small cup from the sink's edge and began to fill it. As he brought the liquid to his lips he smiled. *On no!* He blacked out and sank back to the floor.

5

INSTITUTE, **WV**

As HENRY and Tori were passing through the gates, he thought about John, the old security guard from the day care. He liked John; the man's soothing demeanor always gave him a sense of security, and his sense of humor was unprecedented as well. Things were different now. The guards were many and their protocol more severe. The guards were a bunch of overzealous thugs, sort of like the TSA at the airports, but entirely redneck.

As they made their way through the second gate, one of the men, brandishing a WHS badge on his uniform, stopped beside Tori and motioned for her to roll the window down.

"I'm gonna need you to step out of the car, Miss.""I

don't think so," Tori retorted, pinching her red blouse together at the neckline.

The young man's chin jutted out. He leered inside and said, "I've got my orders. Now you can get out, or you can sit in the car the rest of the day. Don't worry, I won't bite. It'll just take a second.

Henry noticed in his mirrors that more of the guards were gathering around the car. A swagger was in every step as they rubbed on the handles of the guns on their hips. There never was much traffic coming in and out of the complex. It was only natural the bored men would overreact at the sight of a pretty girl. Still, Henry wasn't much for compassion these days. Besides, the look on Tori's face told him she was about to freak out. Something about the man reminded him of his brother, Jimmy, who he hoped he would never see again. He never heard what happened after that night. The leering man was licking his lips like he was about to be fed a barbeque pork chop, and it was more than Henry could stand.

Henry pulled out his phone and texted a message.

"Come on, Lady," the guard urged. "Don't make me use any force, but I will if I have to."

Tori remained rigid and silent. *She's gonna freak out.*

"Looks like she's got something to hide, fellas," the guard said as two other guards began to close in. "Looks like we better pat them both down." He pulled out his night stick and stuck the nose of it inside the window. "You two better get out ... now."

"You're making a mistake ... uh," Henry put on his glasses as he searched for the name tag on the man's shirt " ... Toby. Yes Toby, you're making a big mistake. You see, we've passed all of your little checks, and if you don't let us in you're going to be going home."

"Is that so? Well, Mister, let me tell you something. I could use the day off, but I ain't going anywhere, not until I search you and this pretty little lady right here. Now, you'll do as I say unless you want me to call my uncle, from the local police department, and have you hauled in." The men snickered. "And I'll take her into my personal custody," He licked his lips. " ...and keep a real close eye on her."

"Toby, do you realize how big of an idiot you are?"

"I suggest you keep your big mouth shut, or I'm gonna take this baton upside your head."

Henry sent out another text message.

"Have it your way, Toby, but I tried to warn you."

Toby laughed and said, "Thanks. Now get out of the car—both of you!"

Henry just shook his head and waited. *Come on. What's going on? Is everyone asleep in there?*

There was a loud clicking sound coming from an outdoor speaker overhead.

"TOBY. YOU'RE FIRED. PACK YOUR SHIT AND GO! AND IF THE REST OF YOU MAKE ASSES OUT OF YOURSELVES, YOU'LL BE HEADING BACK TO THE UNEMPLOYMENT OFFICE AS WELL!"

CLICK

Toby looked like someone just shot his dog as the last gate rattled open and Henry drove through.

"You okay?" Henry said to Tori, rubbing her knee.

"Yes, I think. But, poor Toby. Who else on earth is going to give that slob a job?"

"Ha! Ha-Haa! Well, it won't be long before they have the zombies working the gates."

Tori was holding her stomach as she giggled and said, "Oh don't say that, please don't say that. WHS Security guards: Better ... Faster ... Smarter ... than plain ole people."

The jokes were just what they needed before the uneasiness settled in. Henry let the car roll to a stop about thirty yards south of the gate they just left. Ahead was the complex, a roughshod campus of cracked pavement, red brick buildings, and long rows of gray warehouses running along the edge of the interior wall as far as the eye could see. Just ahead was a six story office building that towered over the rest of the campus. The parking lot surrounding the building was vacant except for about a dozen cars.

Henry pushed down on the accelerator and let the car slowly roll over the road towards the back of the complex. He used to come here often, to the complex, back when it was a thriving center for the rehabilitation of many folks in the community. The patients came from all over to be trained by a dutiful staff and refit to function and prosper within society. There was a boarded up entrance to a gymnasium where he used to play basketball games, swim, and even bowl. He remembered the cafeteria, the way it had been, thriving with happy faces and hungry people enjoying a hot meal. They had made the best pizza and home-made biscuits there. Now, the patios where he and his friends used to eat were overgrown with vines creeping up over the walls.

"What a waste," he said.

"What do you mean, Honey?" Tori asked.

"Aw, it's just that I used to come here as a kid, with my mom. It was awesome, like a giant playground. It's just a shame seeing it decaying like this. I mean, you see that rickety gazebo over there?" He pointed up the road to an overgrown patch of grass where a wooden gazebo had collapsed inside on itself.

Tori patted his arm. "I see it, Sugar, I see it just fine. You okay?"

Henry's tongue clove to the roof of his mouth as he fought back his tears.

"I had an uncle; he stayed here. I mean as a patient; he needed help. It was my mom's brother. Anyway, he had some problems, some had ones with drugs and alcohol and Lord knows what else. Well, he and I, we ..." he voice trailed off.

"It's okay, you can tell me. Just let it out."

The warmth of her soft hand gave him the strength he needed.

"We built it. It took two weeks, but we did it. It was one of the best days of my life when we all sat in there and ate. Mom made the best ham salad sandwiches and lemonade. The folks in the cafeteria even brought us some cookies and ice cream." He wiped the tears from his eyes. "It was just a great day ... for all of us."

Jimmy had been there, too, but he didn't want to say it. He could only assume Tori figured so much. It was hard to believe that his life, once so simple and perfect, had turned into what it was now.

"Well Henry, it's a shame," Tori remarked, patting his knee as they stared at the gazebo.

"I know. I guess ... I guess we just didn't do a very good job."

Tori burst out into laughter, and it wasn't long before he followed suit. One thing that the pair had managed to survive on the past few months was a sense of humor. If they couldn't find a way to laugh, at least once a day, they wouldn't have made it this long.

"Funny, why haven't you ever told me that before?"

"I don't know, I guess I just didn't want to think about it. I guess I needed to share that with someone, someone special that is." He squeezed her hand.

"Oh Henry, give me a kiss."

He pressed his lips against hers, and within seconds his sadness was washed away with elation. He didn't care who saw, either, but the complex was like a graveyard, and besides, they were both adults.

HONK! They both jumped as Tori pinned him back against the steering wheel.

"Geez, that scared the poop out of me," Tori said.

"Wow Henry, you really surprised me with that kiss, too. It was one of your better ones; I'll say that, but we're gonna have to go."

"Why? I mean, no one will know. I'm trying to be more adventurous here," he said, pulling her back towards him.

"I know, and I appreciate it. I'm sure I'll regret it, too, but I think I just peed myself, so we need to go."

Henry pushed his glasses back up on his face, blushing, and said, "Oh, okay."

He put the car back in gear and took a deep breath. He wasn't even sure what he was doing right now as it was almost like he was having an out of body experience. He needed to get his head back on straight; he was beginning to feel like he was falling apart. *What am I doing?*

Tori was fixing her lipstick in the mirror when she asked, "So, if you don't mind me asking, what ever happened to your uncle?"

"Uh ... well, a few years before the zombies came they released him, and we never saw or heard from him again."

"That's sad. What do you think happened?"

"He used to talk about going to Korea a lot. Maybe he went there. I don't know," he said with a shrug.

"Did you ever try to look him up?"

"Sure, a few times, but no luck."

"Does it bother you?" she asked.

Henry stopped the car.

"Er ... no, but I'll tell you what does."

"What," she said as she checked her lips in the mirror.

"Zombies walking around on the loose like human beings. Roll up your window, Tori. Roll it up!"

Tori gasped as she pressed the window button.

Stupefied, Henry watched two zombies lumbering his way. One was pushing a lawnmower. The other was dragging a rake.

"You've got to be kidding me."

6

WASHINGTON, DC

JACK LIFTED his custom laptop and flipped open the screen, bringing the monitor to life. It was one of the perks of the WHS, the latest in computer technology. His busy fingers tapped on the screen as he began loading up data files of information that only a handful of people in the entire world had ever seen.

"What are you doing, Jack? Are you doing to give me a PowerPoint presentation? You know I hate those things. Remember the last time ... I think the Senators Grose and Sears were about to die in the middle of your presentation. I still don't know who all of these people are that read and write bills all day long."

Jack laughed at the remark as a spark awakened behind his green eyes. "Yeah right. Those guys don't read or write those bills. Some old man told me that once, not so long ago."

"Ha, ha ... you remember that, do you? How old were you, twelve? I could've sworn you weren't listening."

"Oh, I was listening alright. And I was ten."

Don reached over and scruffed up the thick brown hair on his head. The older man was smiling as his gray eyes set themselves on the images on the screen. "I hope you don't want me to read all of that. My glasses are in the car, after all. Speaking of which ... you want some coffee or something? I can have my driver bring over my Thermos. He's really good at that."

Jack gave him a funny look and said, "How many Thermoses do you have in there?"

"As many as I tell him to prepare."

"You really are a piece of work, Uncle Don."

"I am, aren't I? Now show me what you got," he said, waving his arm up in the air. His armed escort made his way over from the car, Thermos in hand. Don closed the black case to his own custom computer, took the canister, twisted off the cup top, and filled it up.

Jack could see the steam rising from the hot beverage from the corner of his eye and said, "Gee, you even filled it yourself. Impressive. You aren't getting soft on me, are you?"

"Some things, a man has to do for himself."

"Huh ... Hey Oliver, you wouldn't happen to have any Mountain Dew in there, would you?"

The man remained stone-faced as he stared out into the horizon, still enjoying his smoke.

Don dismissed the man with a nod saying, "Thanks Oliver, and don't pay my nephew any mind. He doesn't understand war-horses like us. Feel free to help yourself; by the way. It's getting chilly out here." Don took a sip and followed it up with a refreshing sigh. "Okay, get on with it. What's the latest?"

"First, it's not a PowerPoint presentation, even though I do have one, but this isn't that. It's just some data I wanted to pull up to refresh my memory in case you insisted on seeing some numbers for yourself."

"Nope, I'll let you handle the numbers. I stopped keeping track of those little things about ten trillion dollars ago. Just give me the results, the testing, or whatever you geeks refer to it as."

Jack shifted in his seat as he cleared his throat and said, "Since the acquisition of the XT Formula we've opened six new research facilities across the country, all of which are well concealed from the general public ... well, from just about everyone, really. Now these are all separate and apart from the day-care facilities, one focusing on one area, and some on the others. One facility in particular is manufacturing the formula, while the others are primarily focused on using the formula for zombie rehabilitation."

"Zombie Rehabilitation, hah. Our employers sure

come up with awfully clever ways of naming their experiments."

"You don't approve?" Jack asked.

"It doesn't matter if I approve or not. I just think it's silly. I mean, when the WHS was created I thought it was the biggest joke in the world. It was crazy enough that the world was turned upside down by zombies, but now you have a group of people trying to sell it to the public as a good thing. And the people are buying it. I'm even buying it, because I have to. I never believed in any of it to begin with."

Jack gave him a curious look and said, "Any of what, exactly?"

Don's face turned a little bit pale as his eyes darted away. He took another drink of coffee. Don started to cough, and one followed louder than the last until finally the fit stopped.

"You okay?" Jack said, patting his uncle on the back.

"Fine, fine, just getting chilly, I guess. Damn, I spilled my coffee," Don said, pulling out a handker-chief and wiping the liquid off his expensive computer case. "Ah, it'll be fine; it's leather."

Jack had the feeling his uncle was trying to avoid his stare, and had changed the subject as his last question seemed to have struck a nerve. A very sinister feeling rose inside him. He wanted to know everything about the zombies. He had put in his time, and he deserved to know. Had his uncle known about the outbreak before it happened? His gut was telling him yes, but Don's expression was a de facto no. Over the years it had always seemed like there was something dark that hung over his uncle's head after the outbreak. He wanted to know what that was. As a senior advisor in Washington for decades, he knew that his uncle knew things, things that only the world's most powerful men and women may or may not know. He wanted to press the issue. *He's getting old. He's gotta tell me more.*

"Now where were we, Jack?"

"Well, you said 'I never believed in any of it to begin with,' and I asked, 'Any of what?' And you were about to say ..."

Don refilled his cup and said, "Oh, I see what you're hinting at. Easy Jack, what I meant was when they first reported the zombie outbreak in Washington, I didn't believe a word of it. I'm almost eighty. I've seen things happen in my lifetime that I never could have imagined as a child. About ten or twenty years ago, I began to believe that just about anything could happen. Cell phones, computers, the Internet. But zombies?" I said. "You've got to be kidding me. To an old Catholic warrior like me, it might as well have been the apocalypse."

The words seemed sincere enough, but the pitch in his uncle's voice wasn't as convincing as it normally was. Jack paid closer attention.

"Now the both of us work for a company that is a

caretaker for zombies. Taking care of my parents before they passed away was one thing, but taking care of over a million zombies ... mindless, useless and dangerous? It's beyond conceivable. It's frightening."

Jack sat at his uncle's side, letting the falling sun warm his face with the last breaths of day. It wasn't so long ago when he wondered if he would ever enjoy another sunset again as he reflected on all of the chaos that struck those many years ago. Now, his life couldn't be any better. He had the zombies to thank for that. *Old people never see the beauty in it.*

"Beautiful evening isn't it?" his uncle said.

"Sure is. You know, this might sound strange, but on days like this I think about Nate McDaniel and how he saved the world."

His uncle nodded and said, "With Zombie Dew of all the ridiculous things."

"Well, if you think that is ridiculous, wait until I tell you what they are using the XT Formula for now!"

"Let me guess, they're going to have zombies counting ballots next."

7

INSTITUTE, WV

HENRY'S first instinct was to jam on the gas pedal and run over the approaching zombies. The pair of undead men moved at less than a mile per hour as they approached, and they were in total oblivion to the danger Henry and his vehicle posed.

"Run em' over, Henry, I hate those damn things!" Tori shouted in his ear.

"Easy Tori, geez, I'm right here," he said, almost pushing her face away.

The zombies' slanted walking gate and slack jaws still turned Henry's blood to ice, despite the fact that he knew he should have nothing to fear. But, here they came, wearing dark green coveralls and hard hats, of all things. He had begun to get used to their presence when he was in the complex before, but after being gone for a while the willies came right back. Now, the last thing he wanted was to have his last remaining prized possession, his classic candy apple red 1968 Mustang, damaged by a zombie pushing a lawn mower. There wasn't a path to go around them. He was in an alley where the office buildings were boarded up on the left and right.

"Crap, I'm gonna have to back up. Are you going to be okay?" he asked Tori.

Tori sat in her seat, wide-eyed and picking her lip, and he could see the goosebumps on her arms.

"Such a fine welcoming committee. I wonder who is responsible for this mess. It better not be Rudy. That moron's always up to something."

Henry nodded. His friend had never been the most reliable of people and had grown quite fond of walking the grounds with the aimless zombies. To make matters worse, the director of the complex seemed to be enamored with Rudy's bizarre ideas of giving the zombies a life of greater meaning. Henry could have slapped himself when he unintentionally pictured himself rebuilding the gazebo with the zombies.

"All right, this is ridiculous. I'll back it up, and we'll just go around to the other side."

As he dropped his car in gear, he caught a glimpse of three more zombies in the rear-view mirror; they had boxed him in.

"Dammit! There are more of them!"

Tori's head whipped around, and she let out a frightened squeak.

Henry blinked hard as he pushed his glasses back up on his face. They all had on green coveralls, white hard hats, and work boots that were scraping and dragging over the ground. One of them was holding a shovel in both hands as his neck bobbed from side to side. Another one had a pair of metal tree-trimming shears with the tip scraping over the ground, but the third one was the most disturbing of them all.

"Is that a chainsaw?" Tori cried.

He nodded his head. The sound of the small motor in the lethal instrument was very distinct in his ears.

WAHHH! WAHHH! WAHHH! WAHHH!

"Geez, it can use that thing. Lock the door Tori!"

"It is locked!"

Henry began jamming his finger into his iPhone as the zombies closed in, step by dreadful step. He set the phone on his dash board and left it on speaker as it rang.

"Henry, maybe we should get out and run! They can't catch us. Geez, where are their supervisors! Where's Rudy? That idiot never keeps an eye on those things!"

As the sun began to dip behind the mountains on the horizon, darkness began to envelope everything. The alley was no longer a short-cut to his office, but rather a haven for the awakening of evil. Tori clutched at his arm as he tried to swallow down his fears. His heart thundered so loudly in his ears that he almost couldn't hear anything else at all. He looked at his phone on the dashboard, uncertain as to whether or not it was even ringing because the sounds of the roaring chainsaw and the sputtering lawnmower were caving his senses in. He looked at Tori. She seemed to be trying to say something to him, but he couldn't comprehend it. His nerves were jammed, and his mind had frozen.

Closer and closer the zombies came, and they were singing the most horrible song.

"Num-num. Num-Num. Num-num ..."

Henry always figured it was only a matter of time before the WHS had him devoured. Had they finally figured him out? Did they decipher Nate McDaniel's code he had received? *CPWWSZH.* It wouldn't have been that hard to figure out: World Humanitarian Society World Population Control. Maybe this was why they kept the zombies around, and now they didn't need him anymore, other than to be a rat in some kind of experiment. Henry rubbed his temples.

"I'm sorry, Tori! I'm sorry, this is my fault!"

Tori was just shaking her head, speechless in the shadow of death.

The recesses of his mind began to regain their purpose as a plethora of scenarios became a puzzle that needed solved inside his mind. They had sent him away, on a vacation, something that was an odd and unexpected surprise. That must have been the plan: to set the trap, plan his death, and get the entire incident recorded. *I bet they're watching right now.* He remembered going over the scan areas of all the security cameras that they had set up before he left. He wondered if he was going to be the first victim or one of the last. How many others had been snuffed out like this. *Rudy!*

He could hear Rudy's voice on the iPhone, but it was a recording, a stupid one.

"I'm sorry, I'm not here right now, I have leaped back in time to stop NBC from canceling Quantum Leap. Please leave a message after the beep, and I'll have my zombie secretary, Chi-Chi, send me the message."

WAHRAAA! WAHRAAA! WAHRAAA! Went the chainsaw.

"Num-num. Num-Num. Num-Num," went the zombies.

"Dammit, don't you have a shotgun in this thing!" Went Tori, honking the horn and screaming like a woman gone mad.

The car was surrounded now, and the darkening silhouettes of the haunting figures pressed along the doors, pinning them in. Henry couldn't even bear to look at their faces now. He wasn't going to give them the satisfaction. He closed his eyes and tried to block out the kaleidoscope of sounds so he could think.

Drive through them you idiot! he thought.

"Run them over you idiot!" Tori screamed as he slammed the car into gear and revved up the engine.

"Shit! He's gonna run us over!" one of the Zombies cried out, jumping out of the way.

Another zombie was knocking on the window saying, "Hey Henry, did you pick up my beer?" It was Rudy's voice.

The ice in Henry's veins turned into fire. He was furious.

"Get—Away—From— My—Car!

He wanted to kill them, every one of them as he took a special note of each and every one as they removed their zombie masks. All of the horrifying sounds were gone now, replaced with uproarious laughter.

"I gotta get back to the security office and see this on video. Man, Henry you should have seen your face!" a big black fella named Rod said.

Henry wanted to knock his block off, but he was pretty sure Rod could easily prevent that from happening, being an EFC fighter and all. Still, he managed to shake his trembling fist at Rod. The big man and a few others just laughed and walked away, hauling off their stuff.

"We'll make a copy and bring it to the party," a woman named Myrtle said as she limped away.

That's when Henry noticed something else, too. In his terror, he had momentarily forgotten about Tori, but she seemed to be doing fine, even with all of the tears in her eyes that were caused by all of her laughing.

"You—You were in on this?" he stammered.

She was still cackling, and he couldn't believe his ears.

"I'm sorry, Lover. It was Rudy's idea. I didn't figure you'd fall for it hook, line, and sinker."

"Hey, roll down your window, Bawk. It's cool, just a little prank. You know, a little 'welcome you back' party. I figured it'd get you back in the swing of things."

Henry felt like a fool as he rolled down the window, but it didn't stop him from grabbing Rudy by the coveralls and pulling his head in.

"Don't ever do that again," Henry warned as he shoved the man back outside.

Tori started rubbing his arm, still chuckling as she said, "Easy, Lover. I'll make it right. Man, you're still shaking."

"Get out."

"What?"

"Get out ... now."

"Fine then, you big baby," she said as she got out and slammed the door so hard it rocked the car on the springs. "I said I was sorry."

Henry began to drive off as he heard Rudy yell, "Hey, leave the beer, man!"

He stopped the car and tossed the twelve pack onto the ground with a crash.

"Ah, Henry, you didn't have to do that."

But Henry didn't hear him as he peeled away. He hadn't been back for five minutes and he already wanted to get away. *This place is sick.*

8

LOCATION UNKNOWN

THE NEXT TIME Nate McDaniel opened his eyes, he was looking into the face of a pretty black woman with a tiny mole on her chin. She seemed familiar for some reason, possibly the nurse he recalled hearing the first time he woke up. His nose and face were both aching now, and he was still starving as he reached up to rub his eyes. The woman's hands were warm and soft when she grabbed his, pushing them back down.

"Easy now, big fella. All that moving is what landed you face first on the floor, and after all the work that Doctor Z did to you, you almost screwed it up. Oooh ... he was furious," she said as she put a warm coffee mug to his lips.

"What is it?" Nate managed to ask.

"Just some warm milk and honey to start with. If you can keep this down, I'll give you something solid, but you have to be still ... cause if you misbehave I'll have to go."

Nate didn't like the way she said that as the horror of her leaving the last time flashed in his memory. She was the only link to what was going on. The warm porcelain felt good on his chin as he took a slurp. He never remembered milk or honey tasting so good.

"Ah ... you like that, don't you. Here, let me prop you up some more so you can finish it," she said, reaching underneath his bed and winding a crank. In a matter of seconds he was almost in a full upright sitting position, and she lifted the cup to his lips again.

He started to reach for the cup, but his arm felt like it weighed a ton, and her eyes glimmered a warning.

She said, "Go ahead, but you better not make a mess. I'm getting tired of cleaning up after you. It's hard to clean the crack of a big man like you, and Honey, let me tell you, you make a pretty big mess for someone that's hardly had anything to eat the past few months.

"Months?" he blurted, spitting up his milk.

Her chestnut eyes filled with fear as she waved her hand at him and said, "I didn't say that. Take care of me, and I'll take care of you." She wiped his chin off. "Trust me, you and me both don't want to upset Mr. Z. No, no, no. I've seen too many people disappear after they cross him. I'd take a room full of zombies over a

room full of him." Nate didn't have anything to say. His
sluggish mind was trolling through a whirlpool of
thoughts. It was hard to concentrate, and his heavy
body was still full of aches and pains. At least the
ravenous pangs of hunger were beginning to subside,
but he was still tortured with the thought ... *Where the
Hell am I?*

She began snapping her fingers in his face.

"Hey, are we good?"

"Huh ... uh, yeah, perfectly."

She tucked the blankets underneath his legs and
said as she eyed him, "Perfectly what?"

"Ma'am?"

"Do I look like and old woman to you?"

"Er ... no?" he said as he set the glass on a small
table by the bedside.

"Do you think I'm pretty?"

"Well, yes."

"Good, then you can call me Rose."

"I couldn't have named you better myself," he said
with a boyish smile.

"Hmmm ... I like that. Keep it up, big fella." She
patted his thigh. "Now, you just stay right there while I
go and warm you up some more milk and honey. And
if you keep talking to me like that, I'll make you a
special treat for later," she said with a wink.

He was smiling as he watched her walk away in her
white scrubs that seemed to enhance her attractive
features, but when she opened the door another wave

of fear crashed over him. What if she didn't come back? Had she put something in his drink? *Please hurry back!* When the door closed, he broke out into a cold sweat as only he and the sound of the rattling air conditioner remained. *Where am I? I've got to get out of here.*

He laid his head back, closed his eyes, and rubbed his temples, trying to recall the last thing he remembered. A beautiful woman was dead in his bed. Drugs were everywhere. That evil little man in black and a barrel of a gun pointed in his face—No, put in his hand. There was a loud gun shot. *Oh my!* It was the last thing he remembered before he blacked out.

"Christy Backwater ...," he muttered. He felt an inner victory for just recalling her name. He took a deep breath as he allowed more of the fog to lift from his brain. He wiggled his toes underneath the stiff cotton sheets, and then he realized he had to pee. Over in the corner of the room was a wooden door with a metal handle, either a closet or a bathroom. The pressure in his groin began to burn, and he figured he had recently been attached to a catheter. *Great.* He started to sit all the way up, ignoring the aching fire that was building in his nose, when he heard the door handle moving. *Thank goodness!* He allowed himself to lean back and close his eyes. *Rose will take care of me.* The tension in his neck eased. *I just have to turn on the charm.*

The door closed.

He said, "I missed you, Rose. It seemed like you were gone forever. Now, I've been good and I didn't move a hair, so are you going to give me some more of your delicious milk and honey, Sweetie?"

"No," a man's deep voice belted out, "I was thinking I'd just punch you in the balls, Asshole."

Nate's entire body shuddered at the first syllable of the deep southern drawl from hell.

"I see you remember me," the man in black said. "What's that smell? *Sniff sniff*. Ah, did you just pee yourself? You did that the last time I came to see you, too. Well, I've smelled worse."

This can't be happening! This can't be happening!

But it was, and why wouldn't it be? After all, this was the last man he had seen before he woke up here. Of course, the man in black could only be the reason he survived, who else would have saved him. He assumed the WHS had something to do with it, even though he didn't really have the time or ability to give it much thought.

He closed his eyes again. *Go away! Go away!* He didn't want to open his eyes, but he did. The nightmare was real. Slowly, his lids opened, and there he was: wearing a black ball cap, mirrored glasses, a burning cigarette, a smirk, a black polo shirt with two bean-pole arms, and a sidearm. His lower lip jutted out below a row of yellow teeth and a thin moustache.

Something ignited inside of Nate McDaniel that gave new strength to his limbs.

The little man hitched his foot up on the bedrail as he dropped a load of tobacco in his bottom lip. "So, Butthole that saved the world, how have you been?"

"You killed Christy. You killed Jeanine! You're the asshole, not me!"

The man in black was unfazed, a cold face almost grinning like a fool. The man blew a ring of smoke his way and said, "Is that so?"

"Yeah ... yeah that's so!"

"So you want to fight me now, Lard Ass?"

"What? What is your problem?"

"I don't like you," the man said, flicking his ashes on his sheets.

"Well, I don't like you either! Dickhead!" As Nate pulled his legs over the side of the bed the door opened again, and a large vulture of a man stepped through. Nate froze. *Doctor Z?*

"Get back in that bed, Son," the man said with the authority of a policeman. "Walker, you better not be harassing the patient."

Nate slid his feet back under the sheets, all but forgetting the man in black. The doctor was wearing a white lab coat and jeans, and featured the long haunting face of a seventy-year-old. His droopy gray eyes guarded a calculating mind full of secrets. Nate wanted nothing to do with this man. Something about him wasn't right.

"Did you do this to my face?"

The doctor walked over and leaned over his face with a pen light, causing Nate to flinch.

"Be still," the doctor said, pushing Nate's eyelids back.

The doctor's breath was fresh with peppermint, and his touch seemed squeaky clean as he massaged his fingers all over Nate's face. Nate grimaced. The doctor took a whiff of air and said, "Did you just pee yourself?"

"No ... well, I guess I did when he came in," he said, sliding his eyes over to Walker.

"Hmph ... were you trying to pee on him?"

It was funny how the doctor said it, but he wasn't sure if he was joking or not.

"M-Maybe," Nate replied.

"Walker, get the nurse back in here to clean him up, will you?"

"Yeh Doc," Walker said as he slipped back outside the room.

The doctor sat down on the edge of Nate's bed and folded his long arms across his lap. He rubbed his cheeks and said, "I bet you're ready for some answers, aren't you Nate?"

"Oh, you think?" Nate said, but he held his tone in check. The doctor just didn't seem like someone he would want to upset.

"Okay, I changed your face. Major reconstructive surgery. It wasn't my idea, those were my orders."

Nate started to speak, but the doctor waved him off.

"Why? Well," he paused, "... we couldn't let you exist anymore. It was too dangerous."

Insanity. He was the man who saved the world, so why would anyone not want him to exist? *Harry!* The man had called him every day for years and was the last person he remembered talking to other than Christy. Was he behind this? Did Harry rescue him, or had it been someone else? His mouth was dry, and he had trouble trying to speak as he shifted in his bed. He could feel the spot of damp pee in his pajama pants begin to cool and stick to his leg. He shifted again.

"Don't worry about it, Nate. I'm a doctor; I'm used to it. Come to think of it, I think I nearly pissed myself the first time I met Walker. That gangly little redneck could scare the wings off a bird. He's like a snake made out of ice that slithers up your leg or down your spine. Be glad he's on our side." The strange doctor patted his leg. "I'll tell you a secret, though: I did piss myself the first time I saw zombies. It was early, and I was just starting my shift in the clinic, tending to a comely woman who had a chest cold." The doctor winked. "My kind of patient. Anyway, next thing I know there is all of this screaming and commotion, and I'm running out to see what in the world is going on. The entire lobby was filled with them, eating my patients and nurses. It looked like something you would see on Mutual of Omaha's Wild Kingdom, when the jackals eat a gazelle, except it wasn't natural ... just horrifying." The doctor dazed off, still rubbing his leg, until Nate reached over and brushed his hand aside.

"At least you made it out and lived long enough to screw up my face."

"True, thanks to my SUV. I ran over about twelve of them that day. I never would have survived without it, that's for sure. And to think my wife, my 3rd wife, had almost talked me into buying a Prius a week earlier. Hah! She didn't make it." The doctor stood back up and sauntered over to the door.

"Hey, where are you going? You haven't told me anything."

The man tapped his Rolex watch and said, "It's my lunch time. I'll let Walker catch you up. I think it's time you got better acquainted with him anyway. You two are going to be spending a lot more time together."

It took a moment for Nate to realize that he was all alone again. The air conditioner still rattled, and the air was stuffy. He shook his head, closed his eyes, and opened them again. He was starting to wonder if any of what just happened really happened at all. He reached over for the mug that he had drank from a few minutes earlier, but it was gone. He didn't remember Rose taking it. He shook his head. Was any of this real?

"NO! What's happening to me?" Only the stale air replied.

9

INSTITUTE, WV

HENRY WASN'T in much of a mood to party, but it was hard to ignore all the laughter he could hear roaring down the hall at his expense. If there were a door he would have closed it, but there wasn't. Instead, he was standing inside an open office layout that was filled with outdated desks and cubicles that were actually made out of wood and plaster. There was a large series of plate windows; something like a press box, overlooking another one of the campus's many courtyards that had his attention. He gazed below at a chain-link fence that enclosed an area that looked like an unkempt city park gone wild.

"BWAW-HA-HA-HA!"

It was Rod from the security team roaring with laughter down the hall.

"LOOK AT HIS FACE! LOOK AT HIS FACE! HENRY, YOU GOT TO SEE YOUR FACE! BWAW-HA-HA!"

Rod was so loud that it seemed like he was in the room with him, but he was almost over on the other side of the building. Myrtle was cackling like a hyena somewhere nearby, and about two or three others were guffawing among the throng. He blocked it out and focused on the morbid procession in the courtyard down below.

Six zombies were at work. One was pushing a lawnmower, and another was pulling a made-for-man plow as the other four stood and seemed to be watching in slack-jawed fascination. *Ridiculous.* Two men in black WHS camouflage suits armed with shot guns were in the area, while two other figures, in WHS issue lab-coats similar to his, were watching the zombies. They looked like figurines on a television screen from where Henry was standing. *What are they up to now?*

Henry headed over to the computer station and looked up into the large monitors. Two small joysticks were pinched in his fingertips as he nimbly panned in and out of the images in the courtyard. *What? Weege and Alice?*

"What are those two doing down there?" he muttered to himself.

"Dude, we have a skeleton crew. All of the complex big wigs are gone. Some big conference or something." It was Rudy. *Great.* Henry could hear him gulping down something, but he didn't bother to turn. "The director is still here, though, hiding somewhere in the other quadrant ..."

Henry was panning in on the zombies now. They didn't seem as horrifying in their forest green jumpers and white hardhats. If he didn't know any better, they'd pass for people, from a distance. He zoomed the camera in for a closer look at the zombies that weren't working at the moment. Each sagging gray face had a harness strapped around its mouth. To Henry, it looked more like a retainer, installed by a mad dentist. He could see that the metal brace was hooked inside the rows of rotting teeth, like a bit for a horse, and that it was tethered to a small battery pack that was strapped over the zombie's shoulders.

"... so, are you still mad? We said we were sorry, Henry. You're just so sensitive over the zombies. I mean, they aren't going anywhere, and we have them under control. Come on, have a beer and relax," Rudy said as he edged closer.

Henry didn't even realize Rudy was still talking. His mind was somewhere else. It seemed there was always a surprise of some sort, a breakthrough, whenever he returned. The last time, his brother had been back and intent on killing them all. They had also started testing the XT Formula, without his consent, for what reasons he would never understand. Now, he was certain, and he checked every camera from every angle, certain that something had been done. Something they didn't want to do while he was here, so they sent him away. This time, he was going to figure it out before the big surprise came.

"Hey Henry, quit pouting and get in here and watch this video!" Rod's hulking frame had entered the room and cast a shadow over the top of Henry and Rudy.

He felt obligated to turn around. The two men were just staring at him as if they were waiting for him to say something. Rudy looked like he hadn't shaved since the last time he left, and his Quantum Leap T-shirt had tightened around his belly. Rod on the other hand was a figure that would have made the local fans of John Henry proud. The big man was one of the few people that Henry enjoyed talking with, even though he did have a very boisterous standard of behavior.

"Okay, hold on."

He glanced back over at the screens and almost laughed as he watched the zombie pushing the lawn-mower almost run over the little man from India, Weege.

"What's that fool doing now?" Rod sat as he stepped behind Henry.

He could see Weege screaming and smacking his hand on the remote control box. Alice had a similar one; much like the ones you would see at parks where folks would fly remote control airplanes. She was laughing under a pile of wavy black hair and over-sized glasses.

Rudy stuck his pudgy finger on the screen and said, "That tool is going to get himself mowed over by a zombie. It'll be the first death of its kind."

"BWAW-HA-HA-HA!" Rod roared, holding his gut as he did so.

Henry slapped Rudy's fingers away from the screen, saying, "Quit touching it. When are you ever going to learn?" he said as he walked away.

"Hey, where you going?" Rod asked.

"Down there," Henry replied.

"Why?" they both asked.

Henry turned around, pulled off his glasses, and said, "Because I'm going to figure out from them what you're not telling me. Unless you want to tell me now?"

Rod and Rudy looked at each other and then back at him. Something was wrong, but if they actually knew about it, it didn't show. Maybe he was paranoid, but everything in his body told him something was wrong. Where was everybody? This wasn't like the day care. This was a full blown operation with racks of shotguns still mounted along the walls. The ammo was in good supply. Even though the complex was run down and not perfectly ideal for their operations, it was still well equipped for any emergency.

"Bawk, we're all good here. It's not like the daycare, not like last time."

Rod got a funny look in his eye and said to Rudy, "What are you talking about? What day care?"

Henry glared at Rudy.

Rudy reached up and slapped Rod on his back and said, "Sorry, Dude; it's classified."

"Classified my ass. If it's something I should know, ya'll better tell me, because if something bad happens and I live to tell about it ... I'm coming after you."

"It's nothing to do with anything here, Rod." Henry said. "Just a bunch of crap we had to go through at our last WHS assignment. Audits and paperwork up to my chin—"

"Don't bullshit me, Henry. I don't like it. Now, I'm going back to the party," Rod said, punching Rudy in the arm as he went.

"OW! Geez, my arm's going numb."

"Good," Henry said as he walked away.

Bleep. Bleep. Bleep.

Henry pulled his phone out and checked the text message with a sigh.

COME TO OUR ROOM NOW. WE HAVE TO TALK.

It was from Tori. Henry knew that storm was coming, and it clearly had his name on it. Casting his head down as he pushed his way into the stairwell, he made his way down to their quarters with a dozen unanswered questions roving around in his mind. His interrogation of Weege and Alice would have to wait.

10

WASHINGTON, DC

"So, you're saying the WHS is trying to contract out the zombies to the federal government to handle grounds keeping services?" Don said, avidly watching the scene on Jack's computer.

The colorful display was a video of over a dozen scientists trying to control the harnesses on the heads of the zombies. One zombie was lurching inside of its stiff joints as it tried to chop up a bush. Obviously fascinated by it all, Jack tapped at the screen and brought up more images.

"Watch this, Uncle Don; isn't it amazing?"

"I'm watching," Don said, covering his mouth as he yawned.

Jack pointed at the screen and said, "See, this is

Doctor Milano, and she has the remote control that manages the head and neck. The retainer in the zombie's mouth allows it to respond to signals. A heavy jolt of electricity sent from that battery pack into the bit in the zombie's mouth will cause it to turn left or right, or go forward."

"What? How on Earth can it do that? Are you sure the WHS has approved this? I mean, that seems pretty cruel, running electricity through a dead guy."

Jack smirked and said. "Frankenstein liked it."

"Ho-ho, funny, Boy, funny. And we know how that story ended. Not exactly how I envisioned spending my retirement days, but I see where you are going with this. Seriously though, how does the zombie know where to go? I mean, just because you run some electricity in it, you shouldn't be able to control where it goes. So does this have something to do with the XT Formula?"

"No, not the XT, but I'm glad you asked. Experiments ... Good old fashioned experiments. Once the zombies were subdued, we could strap them down on a table and run tests. As it turns out, there is still a living network of wires er ... well veins ... inside them. We just had to figure out how to manipulate them. Since the zombies are unconscious, so to speak, and they feel no pain, we were able to dig into their brains and rewire them."

Don refilled his coffee and brought it to his mouth

as he said, "So, instead of killing them all, were are going spend millions of—"

"Billions."

"Okay ... Billions of dollars so that we can have 24-hour gardeners. Sheesh. So let me picture this: I'm driving to my office, and instead of seeing a human being watering the lawns and planting the flowers, I'm going to see a zombie that thrives off of a steady diet of Zombie Dew. I mean, people need jobs still, don't they? Won't this cost a lot more than just paying regular ole' people?"

Jack hadn't really given it much thought. He only cared about what was going on in his little world in the WHS and not so much what was going on elsewhere. So far as he was concerned, the flowers took care of themselves. It had never occurred to him that people actually did it.

"Well, I guess it's hard to find people to do those types of jobs," Jack replied. "Besides, the zombies can probably work at night, and no one will ever know that they are there. Right?"

Don huffed as he got up off the bench and started pacing around it.

"I like seeing people in the gardens. I like seeing people anywhere, especially since the Zombies almost ate all of us just a few years ago. Why would the WHS think that people want to see zombies doing what normal people could do? What else are you going to train them to do, be lifeguards?"

"Uncle Don, this is just an early phase. I mean, we really have a long way to go before we replace people."

Don's face began to whiten as his jaw dropped.

Whoops. "I mean, the zombies are only going to do so much. The WHS just wants to show the world that the zombies aren't such a big threat anymore."

Don shook his head.

"Oh, I see, they want to put on a good show. A *humanitarian* effort. Put the zombies on display in some type of zoo so the world can see what a positive impact they can have on society. Seriously Jack, is this what the WHS has you doing? I thought they were trying to cure them, not turn them into appliances."

Jack watched his uncle pace back and forth, his face creased in deep thought. He figured it was a generational thing. Jack had grown up with zombies all of his life. There had been video games, festivals, television shows, and movies aplenty even before the zombie outbreak occurred. When the zombies came, it wasn't a surprise for some, so much as it was an expectation. Jack even knew some people who had let the zombies take them, and he'd be lying to himself if he said he didn't wish to encounter one that was someone he once knew. Still, he was more than curious as to where the zombies came from. The more he played along with the WHS and the harder he worked trying get up the ladder, the sooner he was certain that he would get his answer one day.

His uncle sat back down beside him, shaking his head.

"Ah, I'm sorry. It's just that the more I know about what the WHS does, the less I understand what the WHS does. This is science fiction. Apocalyptic. I know history, and nothing, I say nothing compares to this," Don said, rapping his knuckle on the computer screen. "We are talking about the dead walking among the living, and we are trying to act like it's normal. I've been acting like it's normal. It's not normal."

"Big paychecks make a lot of things seem normal," Jack commented.

He could feel his uncle bristle at his side. Perhaps he had crossed the line. *What's going on with him?* His uncle's current rambling was uncharacteristic, and he couldn't ever remember seeing him pace before. Uncle Don was like a mighty dam that held back the flood waters in the most chaotic situations. Now the old man was carrying on like the world was going to end. It was making him a little bit nervous. Why would his uncle care if zombies pushed lawnmowers or not? So what.

"Money doesn't give you peace of mind, just temporary comfort. Jack, I'm in the position I'm in for one reason ... to protect the only thing that is dear to me ... my family. I'm ...," he grabbed Jack by the shoulder, "*We're* lucky ones, to still have our family. But there is no guarantee we'll still have them with us tomorrow."

Jack patted his uncle's hand and said, "Thanks. I appreciate all that you have done for me and Angie.

But, really, what's the big deal about using some zombies for cleaning up around here? I mean, we can't just kill them."

His uncle began pulling at his chin hairs and started taking deep breaths through his nose as he watched a flock of ducks heading south. Jack had never been farther south than he was right now, but the stiff winds prompted some thoughts about sunny beaches in Florida.

Don spoke:

"Jack, with government, it always starts as something small; an alleged act of sympathy and compassion in the name of some noble cause. But when you plant an evil seed—and you water it—it grows like a weed and spreads as fast as a forest fire."

"How can a mindless thing be evil?"

Don almost gaped as his statement.

"Anything that takes a human life without fear or remorse is evil, Jack, especially when it eats them. What did they teach you in college, anyway?"

"I'm just looking at it from the zombie's point of view."

Don laughed out loud as he held his hand to his head and said, "Their point of view? They don't have a point of view. They don't have a mind."

His uncle was becoming winded as he spoke, and he began waving his arm overhead. Jack's heart jumped in his chest.

"Uncle Don!? Uncle Don, are you alright? Is it a heart attack?"

Oliver, the bodyguard, was at his uncle's side and holding out a small plastic canister. Don grabbed the inhaler and sucked the mist into his mouth.

"Is there anything I can do?" Jack said as he scooted over closer. His own heart was thumping behind his temples. He had never seen his uncle in such bad shape before. His uncle took another puff and waved him off. Then a fit of coughing followed. "Do something, Oliver!"

"He's fine. It's just an asthma attack. Just give him a few seconds. What did you say to him, anyway?"

Jack wasn't paying Oliver any mind, though; his thoughts were only on his uncle.

"I'm fine," Don managed to croak out. "I'm okay; it happens. Thanks, Oliver," he said, handing the man back the inhaler.

"Shouldn't you keep that in your pocket?" Jack suggested.

"No," Don grinned, "I like to live dangerously. Now where were we? Oh I remember. Hey Oliver, Jack was just telling me about the zombies' point ... of ... view. Care to listen in?"

Oliver glared at Jack, shook his grim face in disgust, and walked away. Jack began to feel uneasy.

"Ah ... he probably wouldn't understand, seeing how zombies killed his wife and children. You see, it's going to be very hard to convince someone that a zombie had a good reason to do that."

Jack felt himself shrinking underneath the twinkling gaze of his uncle. He was only reiterating what he had learned from the zombie psychology courses he took in college and from the training he had received from the WHS. He felt like a fool at the moment as he looked away from his uncle.

"Sorry, Uncle Don. I didn't mean to upset you. Are you okay now?" he said, finding the courage to look back. *He's getting old, but I've got to be tougher than him. Shake it off. He's weak.*

"Of course, and so is Oliver. Now, honestly Jack, do you really think that zombies can actually do good things? I'm not talking about with our help. I'm talking about doing good things of their own free will?

"I suppose not. But, they're making progress. Maybe. The XT Formula is allowing us to do some amazing things."

Don huffed, coughed a little more, and took another drink of coffee.

"Well, this is what I've been waiting for. I've been hearing about things with the XT and —"

"You have? When?" Jack said, sounding disappointed.

"Easy now, I've only heard that you've been overseeing some breakthroughs. I don't know what they are because I wanted to hear it from you first. That's why we're here. Now show me what you got."

Jack was excited. It was something like the first time he took his favorite toy, Buzz Lightyear, to school for show and tell. His nimble fingers were quick at work when an image emerged. It was a view of a room full of zombies that panned back and forth in a quirky pattern. It seemed as if the person holding the camera wasn't really paying any attention to what they were doing. The picture on the screen slowly rolled to the left or right, up and down, back and forth. The slack-jawed faces of the zombies—men and women of all sizes and colors—filled the hangar-like room, at least a dozen of them, each just as fascinating to Jack as the other.

"This is making me nauseous. You need to fire that camera-man," Don said, taking another slurp of coffee.

"It's not a camera-man; it's a zombie," Jack said with a smile.

"What? Are you telling me the WHS is spending money to create zombie paparazzi?"

Jack bursted out laughing.

"No, no, Uncle Don. The zombie isn't holding the camera. The zombie is the camera. What you are looking at is the view through the eyes of a zombie."

All Jack heard was his uncle's coffee cup clattering on the pavement.

11

LOCATION UNKNOWN

HE WAS OKAY, just humiliated, but it was worth it just to see another human being in the room with him again. Nate felt no shame as he sat in a wheel chair, naked, while Rose wiped him down and helped him change his clothes. His hard gaze remained fixed on Walker, who was leaning back in a corner with a lit cigarette dangling from his mouth.

"Aren't there any rules against that?" he said, nodding at Walker.

"Against what?" Walker replied.

Rose rolled her eyes as she stuffed his dirty clothes into a plastic bag and slung them in the corner.

"Smoking, Dickhead."

Walker sucked on his cigarette and laughed as he flicked is ashes in the floor.

Rose said, "Walker, quit that. You know I have to clean that up."

"Ah, I'm sorry Rose, I forgot," he said, rubbing the ashes into the tiled floor with his booted toe.

"I'd hate to see where you live," she said as she helped Nate back into his bed.

His stomach gave a loud growl.

"Oh, I'll be right back with your Milk and Honey," Rose said, pinching his cheek.

Nate sat in the bed and continued his glare into the mirrored eyes of the man in black. He hated the man. One of the most vivid memories he had was of the man taking out a shotgun and blowing away his fiancé Jeanine's face. Instinctively, his hand went to his chest.

"Feeling sentimental, are we?" Walker said, dangling from his hand the necklace that Jeanine had given Nate.

"Hey!"

Walker flung the necklace, hitting him square in the face. The gold metal was warm as he inspected it. It was his, the tiny figurine of Jesus on the cross with every detail in place that he remembered. He let out a relived sigh as he began to realize that he was alive, and everything around him was not some distorted dream. "I suppose I have you to thank for this," he said quietly.

"I suppose so," Walker said as he walked over and sat in the wheel chair.

"Not you, Douche Bag—Jesus!"

"Oh ..." Walker said as he began rolling back and forth in the wheel chair. "My uncle used to ride one of these. Pretty cool."

Nate put the cross back around his neck and shook his head. *Psychotic idiot!*

Rose made her way back into the room, sat along the edge of the bed, and handed Nate the warm cup of milk. It was the same one he remembered from earlier, marked in blue and gold lettering, with a small chip along the rim.

"When did you take this?"

"I didn't," Rose said, "he did."

A memory bulb popped inside Nate's mind as the image of Walker spitting in his favorite coffee cup came to life. He remembered now, like it was just seconds ago. He'd been drugged, paralyzed as a pair of strong hangs held him up like a doll. Walker sat before him, calling him names, mocking him and spitting tobacco juice in his mug. He drew his mug-filled hand back.

"Stop it, Nate; you don't want to do that," Rose warned.

"He's a murderer, Rose! He's a bastard murdering creep!"

Tears were rolling from his eyes and soaking into the wiry hairs of his beard. His arm was quaking, and the liquid began to spill onto the sheets. Rose took the mug from him and rubbed his face like he was a little boy.

"Nate," she said softly, "He's not a murderer, and I shouldn't be the one to tell you this," she cleared her throat as she gave a scornful look at Walker, "but he's the man who brought you to us. He saved your life."

Nate was looking into her eyes, searching for lies and deceit, but he only saw the truth. The truth was something that he had become obsessed with over the past couple of years, but if all of his time representing the WHS taught him anything, it was that truth was hard to find. He looked over at Walker. The man's head was cast down, elbows on his knees, blowing smoke rings at the floor.

"Nah, I don't believe it. He killed Christy. I saw him. Why would he kill Christy?" he said, searching Rose's face for an answer.

She looked over at the man in the wheel chair and cleared her throat.

Walker didn't respond.

She did it again.

"Okay Rose, you don't have to yell," Walker said as he stood back up and faced Nate. "You want to know why Christy was killed? Do you?"

"Yes!"

"Because she was about to kill you, Dumbass! There, I said it, Rose. Happy?"

"No, well yes, but you need to explain."

Nate's mind spun like a blender. Why in the world would Christy kill anyone? Why would anyone want to kill him? It had to be a lie.

"LIAR!" he screamed.

"I told you he was an idiot. How am I supposed to work with an idiot?"

Nate felt Rose take his hand in hers as she said, "I'll explain, Nate. Walker isn't much of a talker, it appears."

"I don't believe you or him!"

Nate was angry and confused. For all he knew, the WHS was behind all of this. Walker was behind all of this. Maybe Harry was on the other side of the door, waiting to surprise him. If he was alive, maybe Christy Backwater was, too. His eyes darted to every nook and cranny of the room, searching for cameras, lenses, anything. He had done the same thing back in his apartment. *This can't be true; it can't be happening.* But, in his heart he knew it was real.

"Nate, I'm going to explain. Just, look at me, and settle down. I have your back, remember."

He nodded. Exhausted, he slumped backward, closed his eyes, and said, "Go ahead. I guess it can't hurt too bad coming from you."

"First, let me tell you about Christy. She was going to kill you. She was a WHS spy of sorts, deep cover. She was going to make it look like an overdose. That's where all the drugs came from. But, being the slut she was, she decided to give you a couple of extra rides, for kicks I guess. You must have been pretty good if she let you live through the night."

A half-smile creased his face as the blood drained from it.

"If it weren't for that, you would've been dead. Our people tipped us off about the plan to have you killed, and we had been watching you. That's where Walker came in. He's the one that came in and took out Christy."

"What about the other guy, the big one that jerked me around like a doll?"

"Oh him. Don't worry about him; he's dead now," Rose said, matter-of-factly.

The room began to feel less like a hospital and more like a morgue as Nate stiffened inside his covers and took another sip of his drink. *I bet that guy's on the other side of the door, just waiting for them to call.*

"You know," Nate said, "it doesn't seem likely that Christy was a spy. I mean, I left her on the bed. She was out cold almost. I find it hard to believe that she was going to take a nap right before she was going to kill me."

"She wasn't asleep, Stupid," Walker said.

"How do you know that?"

"We were in the closet the whole time, you know, the one that was almost as big as your bedroom. It was a great hiding spot." Walker huffed some smoke. "And she was watching you the entire time after you left. Not a minute passed before she was on the move, but I could see the whites of her eyes as I popped her in the head."

Nate shuddered inside at the callousness of the statement. The man was nothing more than a stone cold killer with a heart of coal.

"You enjoy killing, don't you?"

"Only when it's evil."

The statement caught Nate off guard.

"Jeanine wasn't evil," he retorted.

"Jeanine was a zombie, Moron, remember? Did you lock her in that cell because you were scared she'd kiss you, or eat you? Besides ... I had my orders."

Nate shook his head and said, "So, you wouldn't have killed her, otherwise?"

As Walker stepped away he said, "It had to be done ... eventually."

Something in the man's voice had the sound of a hint of compassion. For all Nate knew, Walker might have had to put his own family down. Even Nate had done that himself, but he had managed to bury those thoughts over the years.

"So, why is my face changed?"

Rose explained to him that Walker and Leo slipped him out of his apartment building in the dark of the storm. It was a lucky thing because the WHS was moving in fast to secure the scene. It wasn't long before the news spread that Nate McDaniel had killed Christy Backwater in a murder suicide.

That's when he retched.

12

INSTITUTE, WV

HENRY SIGHED JUST OUTSIDE of his and Tori's room. His mind recalled the last time they had a big fight, a little over a week ago. Tori had been upset over her uncooked food in a restaurant and on the very cusp of making a scene when Henry suggested that she 'settle down.' And she had, sitting quietly in her chair, steaming within like a baked potato while he paid the bill. Every footstep he took back to the car left him feeling as if he was closing in on his own grave. She hadn't even given him time to open her door as she jerked it open and slammed it shut. He hated that. Calmly, he entered his vehicle and began to drive out of the parking lot. As soon as they had made their way up the interstate ramp, she had let him have it. Hurricane Tori had arrived with all of the fury of an Italian army. He could swear his ears had been ringing after the chewing out he had taken, but he'd survived.

I'm sorry. I'm sorry. I'm sorry.

Those words would have to be the first ones to cross his lips, as there weren't any flower shops available. He backed away from the door. *I've got more important things to do.* He could always claim he had overlooked her text, or that his phone's battery was dead. He looked at the peephole. *She probably hasn't seen me yet.* He began pacing back and forth in the dormitory hall that once was a thriving living space for many students. His uncle used to live just one floor above. He stopped in front of the door again, pushed his glasses back on his nose, and rubbed his sweaty hands on his slacks.

He hadn't given much thought to what he had done by throwing her out of the car, so to speak. But didn't he have every right to be angry? She was the one that should be begging for his forgiveness, not him, for getting mad, but Tori wasn't the most reasonable person. No, she was a passionate creature whose heart was always exposed. He started to creep away. *Everyone's going to hear her screaming at me.*

"Get in here, Henry! I already saw you through the peephole," she shouted from somewhere inside the room.

There was no turning back now.

"Now!"

As his hand closed around the knob, he took a deep breath and stepped inside. It was dim, but the smell of her sweet perfume hung heavy in the air. His eyes darted all over the room, but Tori was nowhere to be found. The bed was made, the closet doors were closed, and the desk was neat and tidy. Everything was in place, except him. He felt very out of place.

His body shuddered as he heard the sound of a commode flush. From behind the closed bathroom door, he heard her voice.

"Have a seat on the bed, Henry. I'll be out to deal with you in a second, even though you didn't show me the same courtesy, but took your time getting down here."

He sat down on the bed and waited for her to come out. Only a small lamp by the bed was lit, but the room seemed darker than normal somehow. *I'm sorry. I'm sorry. I'm sorry.* It was the only way to diffuse her ... he hoped.

When she emerged from the bathroom, every drop of blood rushed from one head to the other. She stood before him like a dark angel. Her thick locks of auburn hair cascaded down her back, and a long pair of silk black gloves reached up to her elbows. That was all she wore as her voluptuous body came closer to his. He could feel the heat begin to rise between them as she came closer. His mouth watered as his eyes met hers that were so seductive, hungry, and dark.

Her voice was bittersweet as she said, "Take your clothes off."

Henry obliged.

"Lie down on the bed, but leave your glasses on."

Henry was lying back on the pillow, allowing her smooth legs to slowly straddle him. He closed his eyes as she pushed herself down on top of him.

"What—"

"Ssssh ... I'll do the talking."

Then she said as the bed began to rock, "I'm sorry. I'm sorry. I'm sorry. I'm sorry ..."

A ride on the world's fastest roller coaster couldn't have been more exciting, but it would have lasted longer. Still, she was just as sweaty as he was when they both sagged onto the bed and held each other tight. Henry was still trying to catch his breath as he said, "I'm sorry, too."

13

LOCATION UNKNOWN

NATE'S HEAD was swimming as he rinsed out his mouth with a bottle of water. *I'm a murderer?* Rose had been trying to explain to him that after the assassination attempt on him failed and he disappeared, the only option the WHS had was to discredit him. It made sense, but still, why did they want to have him killed? He was harmless. He did whatever it was they told him to do. He wiped his mouth off on the washcloth, tossed it to the floor, and said, "Okay Rose, tell me, why did they want to kill me?"

She squeezed his hand and began.

"Nate, almost a year ago you accidentally pried into one of the greatest conspiracies of all time. Before the WHS was formed, they were little more than some government program that did research on Paranormal activities: ghosts, vampires, werewolves, mummies, I mean all kinds of fantasy stuff. As it turns out, that was just a cover for another black operation that did biological and genetic research on people ... living people."

"That's great. Is that where I am now?" Nate asked.

"No, but I'll get to that. This agency created a biochemical weapon—highly contagious—that could be passed from saliva into the blood stream. This organization, along with our powerful leadership here in America—"

"Ah, I haven't been deported; that's good. I know I must be at most ten miles from a Taco Bell."

Rose rolled her eyes.

"As I was saying, America and the UN came up with a brilliant idea for population control. They created zombies and turned them loose in the most populated cities in the world. As you know, it spread like fire, wiping out over a billion people before you sent the Tweet that saved the world."

"Ah the good ole' days," Nate said with a laugh.

"You don't believe me, do you?" she said with a grim look on her face.

"Do you have any proof?"

"Not that I can show you."

"Then I don't believe you, Rose, so moving on, why did they want to wipe out the world? How did they plan on stopping the virus to begin with? Humor me."

Walker stepped into his view and said, "I'll take it from here, Rose. Okay, Turd, I'll tell you why."

Nate stared at the man, hypnotized by his words. Walker's voice drew him in like a moth to a flame as the deep Southern voice rolled from his tongue like honey. The brash tone was gone, replaced by something almost poetic, in a redneck sort of way.

"Okay," Nate said, without realizing he had even spoken.

"Seven billion people and with a billion more, the powers that be won't be able to control them. I mean what are you going to do when you run out of food, water, medicine and the like? The brilliance of the world leaders was to kill people rather than let nature take its course. Think about it. People are living longer and longer. There isn't so much famine or disease, and even the death counts from war are down. It's pretty much up to natural disasters to slow down the population."

Nate shrugged as he finished off his milk and honey, and said, "That was wonderful, Rose. Can I have some more?"

"I'll be right back," she said with a wink.

"But—?"

"Settle down. I won't shoot you, Idiot."

"Why do you keep insulting me?"

He could tell Walker's stone cold face wasn't going to give him an answer to that.

"Okay, Walker, so we have too many people, and

they created zombies, and they want to create a new world with less people. Why not have a nuclear war?"

Walker put his booted foot up on the bed, rubbed the toes with the washcloth he'd discarded earlier, and said, "Because of all the fallout. You can't spend time at the beach in Malibu if there's a nuclear winter ... Idiot."

Nate was smarter than this. As the veil of fog began to lift from his mind, he began trying to put things together. Greed, power, and control. Sure, he could buy that, but someone, somewhere was pulling all of the strings. The question was, who? The whole idea had to start somewhere.

"I'm not buying it. I just don't think anybody could pull it off. Not like you said, anyway."

"You honestly think this is all an accident? Now, think about that. The zombies showed up all over the world, not in just one place."

"So who did it, then? I mean, you say the WHS, but who is really behind the WHS, and where in the hell am I, anyway?"

"You are safe; that's all that matters," Rose said as she re-entered the room.

"What do you mean, I'm 'safe'? Safe from what, zombies? The WHS? Why did you do all this to me?"

Nate could see Rose's light brown eyes reflecting from Walker's mirrored glasses. There was a hint of fear in them. Walker shrugged and continued rubbing spit into his black leather boot.

"Nate, you are a hero."

"So I've been told, but now I'm a murderer, so I don't see how that helps my situation now."

She patted his hand and said, "Just take a second and think about why you are here, right now."

He tugged as the short hairs on his beard. It was a new sensation to him, playing with an unfamiliar face. *I've never had a beard before.*

"I'm here because you guys brought me here," he retorted.

"I told you he wasn't that smart. It took him seven seconds to answer that question," Walker said, switching to polish his other boot.

Nate rolled his eyes and said, "Do that somewhere else, G.I. Scarecrow!"

Walker let out a laugh.

Rose continued saying, "Why do you think we brought you here? We could have let you die. Walker and Leo, God rest his soul, risked their lives for you."

Nate's eyes narrowed.

"So you say."

"Why then, Nate?"

"Because I'm a hero?" he said, with a funny look of uncertainty.

"Bingo, Dickwad," Walker said as he resumed his place back in the wheel chair.

"Nate, you stopped one of the biggest conspiracies of all time and saved millions of lives, maybe billions.

People love you. I love you. Walker loves you, even though he won't admit it."

"Hah," Nate said, noticing Walker's face was downcast toward the floor.

"Doctor Z loves you."

"The guy that hit you?"

Rose blanched.

"You saw that?" she asked, rubbing her cheek.

He nodded.

"Well, don't worry about that, Nate. I can take care of myself. He's just different. Just does a lot of things before he realizes he did them. It's okay." She rubbed his ankle and said, "But it's awful sweet of you to care."

Her touch was as soothing as her honey and milk. He leaned back, and his eyes became heavy. He yawned. His face started to ache.

"Okay, everybody loves me, but what does that have to do with anything?"

"Nate, we're WHS insiders. Some of us work for them, but we don't like them. They're evil."

"Aren't all government entities?" he said.

"No, but this one is. Listen Nate, when some of our insiders figured out you were being terminated, we became furious. There's a lot of people that work in the WHS just because of you, because—"

"I know, they love me."

"They were loyal to you, and because of you they wanted to help the zombies, but they were misled. The WHS couldn't care less about the zombies. They only want to control the people with the zombies. Think about it: they've taken billions in estates to fund their projects. The zombies' property was seized in that bogus zombie bill that stated all properties belonging to the zombies will go towards the cure and prevention of zombies."

"It's bullshit," Walker added.

Rose nodded. "And now they went and pegged you for a murder. You want to know something, Nate?"

"Anything believable would be nice."

"Seventy-five out of one hundred people believe you are still alive and you didn't kill Christy Backwater."

"Now that, I believe ... sort of." The tightness in his chest began to subside. "Why?"

"Conspiracy. The bogus funeral they threw for you, closed coffin and all, didn't settle with the American public very well. Well, most of the world as a matter of fact."

"Except for the Euro-trash. The Norwegians—like me—were pretty sure you did it," Walker laughed as he lit another cigarette. "Most of Scandinavia, too."

"So you think of yourself as trash? Me, too."

Walker blew a smoke ring his way and said, "Well, at least I know who I am when I look in the mirror every day."

Nate looked back at Rose and said, "I thought you said he loved me?"

"Oh he does; he's just got a funny way of showing it."

Rose's voice was like a mother's, telling a child a bedtime story. He felt his energy begin to ebb.

Rose said, "I think you need more rest. We'll come back."

It was hard to say no. He didn't want to fight drowsiness, so he motioned for her to continue on.

"Okay, so you guys saved me. I still have a following, and some of you have risked your lives to protect me. But, now you've changed my face, I guess so you can hide me. I mean, wouldn't it make more sense to let me go out in public and debunk the entire thing?"

"You'd be dead," Walker added.

"True, but we could go viral and expose them."

"You'd be dead, Stupid, and we'd be dead, too."

"Oh," he said, scratching his beard. He was getting used to it. "So, you changed my face to hide me, so other people don't know me."

"Yes," Rose said.

"Kinda like protective custody, huh?"

"Exactly. But they are looking for you, Nate. One slip up and this operation is gone, and it's the only operation that can stop them."

"Stop them from doing what? They have all of the power and control it seems. What else are they going to do with the zombie funds?"

"It's going toward other things, more sinister things."

"We'll what could be more sinister than planning a worldwide genocide with zombies?"

He could feel Walker's mirrored eyes on him, and his blood turned to ice when she said:

"Another zombie outbreak."

14

INSTITUTE, **WV**

"HENRY, I swear, nothing has happened. Everything is just like it was when you left," Weege said.

Henry and Tori had both made their way down to the field where Weege and Alice were busy rounding up the docile zombies. His good friend from Dubai, Weege, was hiding something, they all were, except Tori. Weege's little eyes were darting back and forth between him and the zombies. Henry kept his eyes focused on the little man as he pressed the issue.

"Have you been here the whole time?" Henry asked.

Weege was fumbling with a remote control that seemed unusually big in his tiny little hands. A zombie woman, clad in the rehab suit and helmet, was slowly spinning around in a circle. Weege banged the remote with his hand and shook it. "Stupid thing."

"Hey, don't call them that," Alice said, glaring at Weege.

"I'm not talking about the zombie; I'm talking about the stupid remote. The zombie's not responding."

Henry had the willies as he stood among a half dozen zombies that walked aimlessly back and forth. One zombie, built like an anvil, pulled a plow the length of the field, only to stall inside the corner of the fence. A couple of others were scraping their boots over the ground, one dragging a rake and the other was biting the end of a small shovel. He felt Tori press her body closer along his side as another woman zombie with a face full of veins and long whispy hair was smacking her lips and groaning "num-num." His stomach recoiled. His hand fell to the .44 magnum revolver at his hip. He didn't take any chances these days. Not with full-grown zombies, anyway.

"Do you really think that's needed," Alice remarked in Henry's direction, with an attitude.

Here we go.

Turning towards her, he replied, "They're always needed when the zombies are around, Alice, and I think it would be wise if you and Weege exercised a bit more caution. Why aren't you two wearing your suits?"

Weege's eyes slid over to Alice and back to him before he turned away.

Alice huffed and said, "The director said we didn't have to wear them if we didn't want to, and I don't think we need to. We haven't ever had a zombie attack inside here, and besides, we have security that will handle any problems. We don't need any cowboys to come to the rescue."

Henry admired Alice's scientific knowledge and appealing looks, but her personality was in need of a major overhaul. He stepped between the two women when he felt Tori stiffen at his side. Tori was very open about her hatred of Alice, and Alice was just as open about her feelings for Tori. He'd better get the train on another course before Alice and Tori collided. He cleared his throat and tried to sound as pleasant as he could.

"Okay, Alice, if the director says you don't have to wear the protection, that is fine. You and Weege can do whatever you want to do with the zombie rehab. As a matter of fact, it looks like you have made an awful lot of progress here. Wow, six zombies, all working towards a common goal," he said, looking around. "This place has never looked better."

Six zombies, millions of dollars spent, and not a single tulip or trimmed tree to show for it. That's the WHS at work.

Alice folded her arms across her chest and said, "My zombies have come a long way, Henry. As a matter of fact, that's the reason I'm going to the WHS Conference—in Aruba—as our facility's top scientist this year, and not you."

"No, it's because you're screwing the director, you four-eyed slut!" Tori yelled.

"You're the one screwing everyone around here, not me," Alice said.

Henry grabbed Tori by the waist and pulled her back, saying, "Let it go."

"Ah, look, the cowboy rescuing the cow pie. How sweet."

Tori pulled away from Henry and pointed her finger in Alice's face.

"I'm going to make you pay, Alice! You zombie-hugger!"

Henry tried to grab Tori as she stormed away. *Best I let her go. Time to straighten this out.*

"Weege, quit screwing with the zombies and get over here," he ordered. "And don't you go anywhere either, Alice. We aren't finished. If you think you can act like a professional for ten minutes and answer my question, I'll be out of your hair in no time. Fair enough?"

Alice was looking at her nails, and Weege was looking at her. It was pretty clear to Henry that Weege was under the woman's spell. Almost every man within the complex was, except for himself. They knew something; Henry was certain of it. *Just wait for it. Weege will bite his nails, and Alice will blow the locks of hair from her eyes.*

"What's new, then? Something is, somewhere."

Neither one of them said anything, but the biting and the blowing began.

"Come on, I've been gone three weeks, and Rudy's already mentioned something classified ..."

Their eyes perked up.

"... so just tell me what it is. I mean, if we've had more zombies dumped on us, you need to let me know. I don't want any more surprises."

Other than the sound of the walking zombies and the words "num-num," the air was dead. Henry rubbed his hands together as a stiff breeze brought him a chill.

"Weege ... Alice, you don't want me to go over the director's head, do you?"

Alice's face darkened as Weege shook his head.

Director Smoot was in charge of the compound, but he answered to Executive Director Galloway, who was over all the compounds, and she didn't like his director. She also just happened to be a former boss of his, as well. She was the one who had bailed Henry, Rudy, Weege, and Tori out in the first place. She didn't like the director, and she didn't like her, either. If anyone knew about any changes in the compound, it would be Linda. She had made it perfectly clear, to him and to Director Smoot, that if he had any trouble all he had to do was call. Maybe now was the time to make that call.

Weege pulled at the hair on the top of his head and

said, "Okay Henry, chill out. We got another zombie, that's all."

"Weege!" Alice shot the little man a glance, causing him to cringe.

"Just one?" Henry asked.

Alice looked at Weege and said, "Well, go ahead, Blabbermouth. He's gonna find out as soon as we let them out in the yard, anyway."

"Them?"

"Uh ... well, two actually. They're in the gymnasium. Um ... they're really cool, Henry. I think you're going to like them."

Alice walked away in disgust.

Weege had a fearful look in his eyes as she stormed out of the gate and across the campus. Henry watched her through the chain link fence as her eyes flitted his way and she started talking on her phone. It left him with a very uneasy feeling.

"Man, I'm glad you're back, Henry. It's been crazy around here. She's a freakin' lunatic."

"Settle down, and tell me what's going on. Two more zombies isn't something they need to keep a big secret about. We move zombies in and out all the time."

Weege scurried over the grounds and picked up the discarded remote controls.

"Here, let me help you with that," he said, grabbing one of the remotes. "Man, these things are heavy." He tossed it up in the air.

"Ah ... don't drop that, it's over a 100K!"

"Alice should have checked it back into inventory, then. She signed for it, didn't she?"

Weege had a look of shame on his face as he shook his head.

"Don't worry about it; just take me to see the new zombies."

Weege smiled.

"Hey Weege, you want us to go ahead and round up the zombies?" said one of the security guards who had just walked over from the other side of the courtyard.

The guard looked like an anvil inside his dark gray zombie-proof suit. The material wasn't as heavy as on the suits at the day cares, but the heavy fiber was virtually bite-proof. Henry's toe began to ache at the thought of when Louie had tried to bite his foot off back at the day care. He nodded at the man, who nodded in return. He wasn't very comfortable around the WHS Security team. They seemed to hold an unspoken grudge against the members of the science team. Their manners and professionalism never seemed sincere.

"Thanks, Jake!" Weege said, grabbing Henry's arm and pulling him along. "Let's lock these up in inventory on our way to the gym. I can't wait to show you our newest members. You're gonna love it."

Henry looked over his shoulder. The two men from the security team were shoving a lanky zombie down a chain-link corridor. It always reminded him of the lion cages they used at the circus. The zombies, as dumb as they were, tended to go straight in the direction you pointed them, especially when there was nowhere else to go. He always felt better after the zombies were locked up. He began to breathe easy again.

About fifteen minutes later, Henry followed Weege into the gymnasium. The air was stuffy, and it smelled like mold along with a faint smell of chlorine. Paint was peeling from the walls, and busted pieces of dropped ceiling were scattered everywhere. The fluorescent lights were out in most of the places that led them down one hallway to the other. Henry couldn't believe it was the same place where he had played basketball only a few years ago. He kicked a piece of broken tile, and it echoed down the hall.

"Why aren't they with the rest of the zombies?"

"They're getting fitted."

"How long have they been here?"

"They got here nine days ago," Weege replied as he turned on a light switch.

The lights clicked on to reveal a small basketball court and several rows of pull-out bleachers. Henry thought of all the times he had tried to dunk on those rims, and he swore they were an inch too high.

"It doesn't take that long to put on the head harness. Why are they still here?"

"They needed special fitting, and the director wanted them separated from the others. He thinks they're special."

Nothing was special about zombies; they had all proved that time and time again. *Must be a relative.*

"Is anyone back here with them?"

"Nope, they're under lock up, and the cameras keep tabs on their whereabouts. You know they're all tracked, anyway. Don't be so paranoid."

"How can you not be? They almost took us out, Weege, and that was just one kid. What's going to happen if the adults go wild?"

"Henry, we have armed men everywhere. Plus, the zombies are all doped up on Zombie Dew, and there hasn't been a zombie attack in years. Chill out. I know you just got back, but you'll get used to it."

He shook his head. Nothing was ever going to make him feel comfortable around the zombies. It just wasn't natural. The XT Formula had given him a glimmer of hope, back at the daycare, and the WHS had led him to believe that he would be a part of the solution again, when they asked him to sign the 5-year contract with them. He was wrong to believe, and the XT Formula, for all of his inquires, had slipped from his grasp. His stepfather Stan was gone, and the legacy with him. Thinking about all of his family that had perished left him empty inside.

He stuck his hands inside his lab-coat pockets and said, "Let's get this over with."

Toward the back of the gymnasium was a padded floor filled with weights and exercise equipment that had been modified for testing the strengths and limitations of the zombies. The crew would harness the zombie's arms and legs to the equipment with thick leather straps and observe them trying to push or pull free. Most of the time, the docile creature would just sit there hour after hour, gazing at nothing, but when the hunger came, the weights would begin to jerk up and down. The zombies were stronger than the average man, with the raw power of an athlete but unhindered by fatigue. He remembered one zombie pulling an entire machine over on top of itself and laughing.

Weege's ferret face was lit up with excitement.

"Here we are."

They were standing in front of a window that was as black as night on the other side. Henry knew that the glass was at least three inches thick, but he still felt like it was going to break at any moment. A heavy door with a magnetic security lock glowed with a tiny red light. It didn't give him any comfort. He began to thirst as he wiped the steamed-up lenses of his glasses on his coat and put them back on.

"Okay, let's see it."

Flick

His heart stopped as he stumbled back. It was the two biggest zombies he had ever seen, and they looked hungry. Every fiber of his being told him to run, but his legs wouldn't move. *This is insane!*

15

Washington, DC

Don Baker had seen many mind-blowing things before in his life, but nothing compared to this. His stomach was turning into knots as his nephew, Jack, explained what he was watching. All of the triumphs of mankind, from the automobile to the nuclear bomb to the Internet, seemed minute in comparison to what he was beholding. The zombie point of view was a disturbing thing, but it fascinated him as nothing ever had before. He was hunched over on the bench as Jack explained.

"It's amazing, what we have learned over the past several months, Don. The XT Serum worked miracles of sorts. The brain function of the zombies went from five percent to just around twenty. The entire nervous system was at our disposal. We could explore the brain from the very top, and down to the bottom of the spine. Since the zombies don't feel, we could do just about anything."

"But, if their nerves are firing, won't they feel pain?" Don inquired.

"Nope. No emotions, either. They're like robots made of flesh and bone. Here, let me have your screen."

"Couldn't you have just used little cameras like our military uses? I'm sure it would have been easier and cost much less."

"We can do both. As a matter of fact, those cameras are back-up, seeing as how the zombie eyes are still in an experimental phase. But it's amazing; the zombie's lens is so superior to the smaller camera lenses. We were even able to make a breakthrough on using the eyes to help guide them. It's sweet!"

The excitement in Jack's voice disturbed Don. The younger man over forty years his junior, seemed to have become obsessed with the amazing world of zombies. Don was carrying enough guilt already for having taken part in the outbreak, and now he had drawn his nephew into some psychotic-thriller world that kept morphing into something else. Don never would have believed the zombies could have wrought the amount of damage they had. It was supposed to be just another big government scare tactic, a little some-thing to keep the world in line. He had been certain that even after the intervention of Nate McDaniel, the plug would be pulled and the world would churn back to normal. But now it was clear the WHS had other plans. And the worst thing was they were clearly plans that he wasn't being included in.

Jack handed him back his computer, saying, "Just watch the screen, Uncle Don."

Don's chin dipped down. On the screen, he could see a cavernous room, something like an aircraft hangar, and it looked like he was jogging. The motion was jerky, but realistic.

"How does this work?"

"Hold on," Jack said as he typed messages. "Ah ... the zombie's entire neural network is wired up to people in a simulator, much like they use in video games. We can control them and have them pick up things, run, and jump. But it's not perfected yet. The optic nerve behind the eye has been wired to send signals back to our systems. Some guy said he got the idea from a movie called 'Inner Space'. Turns out it was a good one. It works.

"I guess they don't blink, either?"

"Huh, never thought about that, but I guess not. Here, watch this. I'm going to send them a message to have the zombie jump.

Don held the screen up to his nose. The picture lifted up, came down and headed for the ground. The screen went black. "What happened?"

"I think it fell. It happens; just wait."

Slowly, the concrete floor came into view, and the image panned back to normal.

"See?" Jack said, "now watch this."

The zombie's hands were smacking together, faster, then slower.

"Can they hear, too?" Don asked.

"No, but that's not a problem. We have a microphone in their suit. Just give it a second."

The claps were more like dull smacks, but audible. Another annoying sound filtered into his ears as well.

"Numma-Numma. Numma-Numma."

Don muted the sound. He couldn't take it anymore. All of the senseless deaths over the world had taken a toll on him. He was too old to get involved with another deranged war for the control of mankind, but he was in too deep. Like a good soldier, he had to play along, not just for his sake, but for the sake of what was left of his own family. Maybe even the sake of humanity, itself. Secretly, he wished someone, somewhere, could put an end to all of the madness. He always had hopes that Nate McDaniel would be the one. After all, he had been warning the man for years, but now he was dead. Oliver returned beside the bench and was holding his overcoat. He yawned as he stood up and slipped it on.

"That's fascinating, Jack. They'll make excellent gardeners," he said

"And soldiers."

"What?"

Jack's voice sounded sinister when he said, "Sit back down, Uncle Don, and I'll show you."

Don reached for his computer and sat back down. He flipped open the cover and blanched.

The picture was inside another warehouse that was filled with over a dozen figures. They all were adorned in combat boots, dark green and black jump suits. A dark metal glinted on their faces.

"Are those zombies or men?"

"Zombies."

"What's on their faces? Are those masks?"

Jack snickered.

"This was one of my brain storms. It's a titanium mask and skull cap I designed. I got the idea from something I saw on Warcraft. Pretty badass, huh."

It was horrifying. The zombies looked like metal skulls with snapping mouths, like gladiators raised from the dead. The zombies moved fast as they stumbled and climbed over top of one another. Don pulled his coat tighter over his chest. The chill breeze of the early evening was suddenly cold.

"Why do they need those helmets?"

"So if they get shot in the head they won't die."

Don grabbed his nephew and said, "Who's going to be shooting at them?"

"The people in the complex."

"What complex?"

"Institute,West Virginia."

16

LOCATION UNKNOWN

ANOTHER ZOMBIE OUTBREAK?

Nate rubbed his eyes. It was the last thing he remembered Rose saying before he drifted off to sleep as exhaustion took over his weakened body. He didn't want to wake up, though; he still just wanted to sleep ... he felt comfortable. His vision was blurred as he rolled his head to the left and to the right and filled his nose with the musty air. He smacked his lips to keep his tongue from probing the inside of his filmy mouth.

What is that?

He heard a crunching sound, and his mouth began to water. The scent of tortilla shells, cooked beef, and taco sauce filled his nose. His eyes snapped open as he lurched up.

Walker was sitting in the wheel chair, stuffing a hard-shell taco into his mouth. Rose was wiping her mouth with a napkin at his side. His stomach made a sound like a croaking bullfrog. She smiled.

"I told you if you were good I'd give you a treat."

She handed him the Taco Bell box. A new Ferrari couldn't have replaced the treasure he now held inside his hands. Licking his lips, he looked at her.

"Go ahead, just don't eat too fast. And easy on the Dew," she said, tapping the large cup on his food tray.

He didn't hear anything she said. He just ate and ate and ate. *If you can die happy, then take me now, Lord.* For the first time in what seemed to be forever, he felt like a complete human again. He thought of his condo in DC: his toys, games, and DVD's. He assumed all of that was gone, but a small apartment in the middle of nowhere would be just fine, if he could just figure out what he had to do to get out of wherever he was.

Walker wadded up his paper wrappers and tossed them into a metal waste basket. The man sucked the remaining fluid from his cup and it sounded like Nate's brain was being sucked out.

"Do you mind? I think it's empty."

Buu-urp! Walker responded as he lit up another cigarette.

Nate wiped his mouth and asked, "So, when is the doctor coming back? Surely he'll want to do more mutilations to me." He rubbed his face. It felt tight, but it didn't ache as much as before. He sat up on the edge of the bed, fully expecting Rose to push him back down, but was greeted with her supporting arms instead.

"Feeling spry, I see," she said, "Go ahead, see what you can do."

He looked at the gritty floor.

"I hope you didn't do the surgery in here.

"I'll get you some slippers," Rose said.

Walker let out a wicked snicker. Nate watched the man pull off his glasses and wipe the mirrored lenses. Their eyes locked as Walker turned into his stare. Nate's impression of Walker took a sudden turn.

"What're you staring at?" the man said as he put his glasses back on. "What's the matter, Big Mouth, cat got yer tongue?"

Nate's tongue clove to the roof of his mouth. He shook his head.

"I just ... I just thought you were older."

The glimpse Nate just had of the man's eyes told a different story from the cold-blooded soldier the man appeared to be. The man's eyes were soft and round, his skin rosy around the cheeks. The grizzled chin, moustache, and sideburns had thrown him off. Walker didn't look more than thirty years old at the most.

"Well, I thought you were smarter," Walker replied.

"How old are you?"

"I'm old enough."

Nate laughed. He figured that killing zombies for a living and smoking non-filtered cigarettes was bound to age a man a decade or two. Something cold slivered down his spine. He never really got a good look at himself. The floor was cold on his feet as he headed for the mirror.

"Don't you need your slippers?"

"Don't you need to graduate from high school?"

Nate was already at the mirror when Rose returned.

She tossed the slippers on the bed and said, "I see you still haven't found your patience."

"Huh?"

But he wasn't really paying any attention. The eyes and hair were the only things that seemed familiar. His nose was smaller, and his chin bigger. His head slowly turned from side to side. He ran his hand along the back of his head. His ears were smaller, and his long earlobes were almost gone. *Is it still me? Maybe without the beard.*

"No razors here, Nate. It's best you kept the beard for now," Rose said. "I like it though, the new chin, too. Your old chin made you look fat ... at least on TV it did." She patted him on the back. "Don't worry: you're still handsome."

"I still think Doc should have turned him into a woman. No one's gonna pay any attention to an ugly girl," Walker commented.

Nate grimaced as he stared into the mirror. It was going to take some getting used to, that much was for sure. *Yep, it could have been worse.* His legs began to tremble, and his head became woozy. Rose rushed to his side and guided him back to the bed.

"Take it easy," she said.

"I'm ... I'm okay." He cleared his throat.

"Rose, I'm grateful that you guys saved me because you felt obligated, but there has to be more to it than that. Is there?" he said in a pleading voice.

She placed a cold compress on the back of his neck and said, "There is."

"Wow, I wasn't expecting that. A direct answer on my first try. Okay then, what is the other reason, or reasons rather, I am here?"

The door opened, and Doctor Z entered with a clipboard in his hands.

"How are you feeling Mr. McDaniel ... er, rather ... Nate?"

"Better."

The doctor made himself comfortable on his bed.

"Well, your vitals are good. Do you have any questions?"

"I was just asking why I was *really* here. I mean, rather than the fact that I'm an awesome hero. I'm of the impression there's much more behind my reconstruction than that." His eyes slid over to Rose. "Oh, and the fact that I'm a murderer."

Rose gasped when the doctor grabbed her by the collar and jerked her face to his.

"What did you say, woman?"

"Hey! Let go of her," Nate cried.

"Nothing you didn't already discuss, Doctor," she managed to say.

Nate didn't notice the smile in her eyes.

"Hmm. Hmm. Hmm," the doctor laughed as he let her go. "Oh Rose, how you stir the blood in me. Will you be a dear and get me some coffee?"

"Certainly, Doctor."

He slapped her on the rump with his clipboard.

"She loves me. I can see it in her eyes. Can't you?" The doctor's eyes were still following her from the room.

What? This weirdo reconstructed my face.

"So, I see you enjoy *hitting on women?*" Nate said.

"Hmmm—Oh, now don't be silly. I could never harm that endearing woman."

Nate wasn't convinced, but he was getting aggravated.

"Okay, on with it. I'm a hero, I'm a murderer, and I am here because why? The real reason."

Walker made his way over to the edge of the bed.

The doctor spoke matter-of-factly.

"Nate, you are the man that saved the world. We all know that, don't we Walker?"

"Yes sir."

"Now, what we need to find out is: 'Who is the man that wants to destroy the world?'"

Nate was at a loss.

"Why ask me? I don't know. If anyone knows I'd figure it would be you guys."

The doctor tucked his hands under his arms and said, "The WHS has many layers, like an onion or the earth, so to speak. We've only been exposed to the middle, which is deep, but not deep enough. What we haven't been able to do is penetrate the core. That's where the answers are. Now, every once in a while something slips out, and if we are lucky, like we were with you, we can learn more about the enemy. But since you disappeared from their radar, the seal around the core has become tighter." He clenched his fist in front of his face.

"Well, I don't think I can help you. I'm pretty sure I know less than you do."

"I'm pretty sure that you know more than you think you do. The WHS has been squabbling since you disappeared. One faction is blaming the other. Our little rescue has splintered parts of the operation, and many of their operations have gone deeper. I think that you've been exposed to more than you realize, Nate. We think you might even know who is in charge of all of this. You might even be able to point them out."

"That's ridiculous."

"So was the thought of Christy Backwater assassinating you. So are zombies. Nate, what can you tell me about a man named Harry?"

The hairs on the nape of his neck stood up.

17

INSTITUTE, **WV**

HENRY STEPPED backward and stumbled to the ground. Horror. Terror. Fear. Instinctively, his hand clutched at his chest. His breathing was heavy. His heart pounded. *Madness!*

"Henry? Henry! Are you okay?" Weege said. "You look like you're having a heart attack. They're all locked up, Henry. They can't hurt us. They're cool!"

The word 'cool' wasn't something he associated with the zombie vocabulary. He sat on the ground, agape. The silent giants behind the thick glass looked like fiends in an aquarium. Their faces were long and terrifying as they meandered with jagged gaits within the small cell. Their heads would have touched the ceiling tiles if they weren't leaning over. Brain eating monsters on stilts was what Henry saw, and his heart recoiled in his chest.

"Weege! Where did they come from?"

"I don't know. The director got them somehow."

Weege's eyes sparkled like lanterns as he tapped on the glass and waved at them.

"Are those basketball uniforms?" Henry asked, rising to his feet. His legs were weak, but the initial shock had subsided.

"Yep."

He edged closer to the glass, looking up at the men. He whirled toward Weege and said, "That's 'Rifle' Rick Braxton and Sam 'The Slam' Jones!"

"In person." Henry tried to rub his eyes, but his glasses got in the way. He loved the NBA, and *Rifle* and *Slam* were well known all-stars. He felt compelled to ask them for autographs. His step-dad Stan would have loved that. A few moments passed as he and Weege stared at the roaming zombies with awe. *This is absurd.*

"So let me guess: we're starting a zombie basketball league now? Are we going to set up a match against the Harlem Globetrotters? I can't imagine what our infamous Director Smoot has in mind Weege, can you?"

"Take it easy Henry. They just got here, and no one's mentioned a basketball team ... yet." Weege smiled.

Henry could see the wheels turning in the little man's head. Weege and Rudy had become more like pets than men since they'd all been forced into service at the WHS rehab facility. Henry'd previously had control over them, but now he was pretty sure his alliance with them wasn't as strong as before. He'd learned it was best to bite his tongue when discussing serious matters with them anymore.

He noticed Weege was texting.

"Hey, what are you doing?"

"Sending a text."

"About what and to who?"

Weege's thumbs stopped. He put the phone inside his lab coat pocket.

"No one, it can wait."

Little rat.

Ring –Ring!

It was Henry's cell phone.

"Hey."

Rudy was on the other line.

"HENRY! Get up here now! I think we have a zombie breach!"

"What? Where?"

"Avoid Quadrant 14. Where are you, anyway?"

"The gym. Hey—"

"Is Weege showing you Slam and Rifle?"

"Yes but—"

"Quit fooling around, Henry, and get up here!"

"Hey, is Tori with—"

The line went dead.

"What is it, Henry?" Weege said.

"Rudy says we have a zombie breach. Quadrant 14. Let's get to security."

"Ah ... I'm sure it's nothing," Weege turned off the lights inside the zombie room. "Night fellas. Man, I can't believe we have NBA all-stars working with us now!"

Henry was dialing Tori as he rushed back toward security. Weege's footsteps were echoing from behind. Fear rose up inside of him despite his efforts to reassure himself that there was more than enough security to take care of things. Then he remembered they weren't fully staffed because of the zombie conference. He had to hurry back to security to make sure all of the protocols had been followed to secure the zombies.

"Hello Henry," Tori said on the other line.

A wave of relief washed over him.

"Are you with Rudy?"

"Yes, I'm safe. You need to hurry back, Henry. These jackholes don't know what they're doing. Rudy's going bonkers."

"Don't worry, I'm almost back to the doors. Have you seen any zombies on the screen?

"No, they won't let me in there. You need to get back and straighten this out. They're talking about a total lockdown."

Henry scanned his card, made his way into the building, and headed inside the elevator.

"I'm on my way up."

He lost the signal as the doors closed.

"I'm sure it's nothing, Henry. Rudy's probably half in the bag. You know how spooky this place gets at night. It's like a ghost town."

True. The complex was like a graveyard for buildings more than anything else. There was a network of dorms and classrooms, a small hospital, a cafeteria, a church chapel, and even a cemetery. The nearby river was notorious for rolling in fog thicker than soup most of the time, too. It all but negated the security cameras outdoors on some days.

The elevator chimed on the 3rd floor, and Henry and Weege were greeted by Tori.

"That fool is freaking me out. Get in there!"

Henry made his way back to the observation room only to be greeted by two sealed metal doors. He scanned his card. It flared green and the doors parted open.

"Hey!" Rudy shouted. "Get Tori and Weege out of here. They aren't authorized, Henry!"

Rudy's eyes were bloodshot, and his clothes and hair were a mess. Rod was nodding his head, and another guard, Myrtle, had her eyes intently on the wall of monitors. He pushed past Rudy, noting the heavy scent of alcohol on his breath.

"Hey Henry, I'm warning you," Rudy said.

Henry faced the man and said, "You're warning me! I'm warning you, Rudy. You're drunk. One more word and I'll have you locked up."

"That's insubordination," Rudy slurred.

"Everybody, who thinks Rudy isn't fit for duty?"

Everyone raised their hands.

Rudy sat down, slumped on the desk, and mumbled something unintelligible.

"Look! Look here, everyone!" Myrtle shouted and pointed at a screen.

Quadrant 14 was a row of cinder-block warehouses in the WHS lab district. It was a separate operation from their rehab facilities. Top secret times ten. So far as Henry knew, it was just storage. Trucks came in and out every so often, but nothing ever appeared to be out of the ordinary.

A shadowy figure was moving along those grounds. Tori gasped.

"Rod, did you dispatch a team?"

"Yep. A fire team's going in to check it out. Got them on the head phones now."

"Can you put them on speaker?"

Rod looked over at Rudy, who was snoring.

"Looks like you're in charge. A good thing, too. I was about to punch a hole through him."

Rod nodded at Myrtle.

The audio came, and Henry could hear heavy breathing. On one screen he could make out a shadowy figure roaming through incoming fog, and on another he could see three members of a security fire team closing in. Tori was clutching at his back as they all gawped at the screen.

Henry could hear the fire team leader over the speakers.

We got him in our sights. What in the world is that?

The security team had flanked the strange figure in front of one large garage door. Henry could make out all the images on a single screen now. The security lights were doing a good job of cutting through the fog.

"What is that?" Rod said. "Is that a zombie or a man?"

Henry couldn't tell. Its movements were stiff and quick. He could make out a mask of some sort on its head, more like a man. It had on a dark jump suit of some sort.

Halt! Put your hands on you head. This is WHS Security, and we have authorization to use deadly force.

Rod spoke into his radio. "Don't hesitate, Jim. If that thing doesn't stand down, disable it. Don't kill. Just take out the legs.

Roger that, Rod.

"Myrtle, can you zoom the camera in any closer?" Henry asked.

"That's all I can do. There should be another WHS Security team from the warehouse quadrant en route. It's their area. All of our zombies are locked up and accounted for. Maybe it's an intruder."

"I've never seen a man move like that. It's a zombie," Henry said.

He wiped his forehead with his sleeve. *This can't be happening.* He could feel the tension building in the room as they all stood mesmerized by the screen. First giant zombies and now this.

"Has anyone notified the director?"

"Rudy did." Myrtle said.

"And?" Henry inquired.

Rod and Myrtle shrugged.

On the monitor, the security team, clad in full zombie gear, had fanned out in front of the zombie.

"Rod, it's a zombie. It has some kind of skull cap on. Looks like a gladiator helmet or something. It's just acting like a typical walker. Is this some kind of prank or something? It better not be. It's pretty screwed up, and I'm gonna bust someone's ass if it is."

Many eyes fell on Rudy's snoring form.

"Hold on! It's having a spasm of some sort."

Henry watched the zombie arc up like it was shot in the back. It rushed the men. Tori and Weege screamed.

BLAM! BLAM! BLAM!

Henry covered his ears.

Rod ripped off his headset. "Dammit!"

The shotgun blasts tore into the zombie, knocking it from its feet. It was difficult to see underneath the blanket of fog.

"Did you see that? Geez, I never seen a zombie move that fast before. Wooo-Weeee! It's dead as a rock now."

There was a pause.

"Jim, you sure it was a zombie? Are you there?"

As he watched the screen, he could see the men

huddle around something. Two of them jumped back, bringing another frightened gasp through the room.

"Yep, it's still moving. Not much left of it, but it's moving. Creepy. The jaws are still snapping like a turtle. Uh ... wait a second. Hey, the garage is opening. Looks like the cavalry's coming ... just a little late is all."

A small wave of zombies burst forth and crashed into the security team.

HELP! GET SOME HELP! HEL ULP—

The sound died. They all stared in horror as the zombies pinned the men under their weight and tore into them with fervor. Henry's worst nightmare had come true. The zombies had been turned loose on them.

"Initiate the lockdown!" He cried. "Secure all floors!"

"No Henry, let's get out of here while there is still time. I don't want to be locked up in here with them," Weege cried.

"We'll be fine in here."

An alarm sounded.

"Just lock this building down. Rod, tell your men to find a bunker and lock down. We don't know what we're dealing with. Weege and Tori, wake up Rudy."

The alarm stopped.

"How'd that happen? Who did that?" he said.

He dialed the director on the desk phone and let it ring on speaker.

"Just let it ring."

The zombies were on the move, like a wave of rioting men.

Chooooooom.

The screens winked out. The lights turned black. The ringing phone went dead.

They stood in the silence of the insecure building with no idea what to do next.

"We're gonna die," Weege said.

18

Washington, DC

JACK WATCHED IN AWE. The men of the security team couldn't withhold the fear that grew in their faces as the zombie rushed forward. It was almost like playing a video game, except the shotgun blasts and screams were so much more real. Unable to hide his fascination, he giggled as the men fought against the hoard only to be barreled over and pushed down into the fog. They couldn't have made it any better in Hollywood. The zombies were on the men like a pack of jackals, tearing off the suits and sinking their faces into the men. The close view of the zombie eyes was a little too close as the image thrashed and jerked like it was on a roller coaster.

"Good Lord, Jack," Don exclaimed, "What are you doing? Those are our people!"

Jack looked over at the distraught features of his uncle and noticed the man had aged another ten years.

"Ah, you know what you always taught me Uncle Don: Don't mess with the WHS. I've got my orders, and I have no choice but to run this op. It's for the greater good. You always told me that ... remember?"

His wide-eyed uncle looked like he had swallowed a toad. For decades, Jack had thought his uncle was as tough as iron and cunning as a shark. Now his uncle had changed. Don looked old, haggard, and weak. The time had come for a strong young man to pick up the banner and lead the charge to bring order back to humanity. No mercy. Just results. And if turning loose a wild pack of zombies on a bunch of men and women was what they wanted, then that was what they were going to get. A show.

Don was pleading:

"Jack, there comes a time in your life that you're going to make choices that you're going to regret. This will be one of them. I didn't bring you in to become a bigger part of this. I brought you in to protect you. These people that are dying have families. Just like me and you."

"I know that. But, we can't all have the life that we want. I consider myself grateful this is happening to them and not me. Besides, they're all loners."

"They're human beings!"

"They're expendable. Just like that other billion you helped wipe out, so what's a dozen or so more? Isn't that what you wanted to begin with?"

Don was silent.

"That's what I thought. Now keep your eye on the screen, Uncle Don. And just so you know, this isn't my first rodeo," Jack said with a wink. "I'm having them cut the power to everything except the security wall and the interior fence. If anything tries to climb that fence, man or zombie, they'll be fried chicken. The security servers have all been switched under our control. Inside the complex, everything is dead except for the emergency lights. All of the zombie shelters are sealed off with magnetic locks, and if you aren't already inside, you won't be getting in. All communications are off unless they hack into our system, but that's not likely. It's on the other side of the wall."

He cleared his throat as he pointed at his screen.

"And if it makes you feel any better, the humans are still armed. They have shotguns, side arms, and plenty of ammo. They have zombie suits, masks, and helmets, so they aren't fish in a barrel. They're just the fish and the zombies the fishermen."

His uncle was as stone-faced as he'd ever been.

"Come on, Don. Now's not the time to get attached to people. You know what is going on. We're the lucky ones. You might as well make the most of it and enjoy the show. You know they're going to want your opinion on this and that you'll have to play along as if you like it, so go ahead and pretend to like it." He cleared his throat again. "Come on, you're making me uneasy."

"Okay, okay," Don grumbled. The older, bigger man pulled his head and shoulders back and flipped open his computer cover. His fiery gaze returned as he stared Jack back in the eye and said, "You want to make it fun, Boy? Then put your money where your mouth is." Don extended his hand. "I'll put twenty thousand dollars that those men and women beat your zombies."

Jack swallowed hard and said, "Well, I hardly see the poi—"

"TWENTY THOUSAND, NEPHEW! That's what it will cost for me to enjoy this. What's the matter? You're not losing your faith in the dead, are you?"

Jack stiffened at the remark and said, "Fine, you're on!"

"Good, then what are your terms?"

"Easy, just one of them has to live until sunrise."

Don had a calculating look in his eyes as he scratched at his chin. Jack wasn't worried, though. The last complex they turned the zombie soldiers loose on ended up being a slaughter. The humans lasted little longer than three hours, and the next sunrise was over twelve hours away. The zombie soldiers were incredible hunters that could smell blood and brains from a mile away, and even if the men managed to disable them, he still held another ace up his sleeve. He smiled. All of those years of online poker in college were going to finally pay off, big.

Don shook his hand and said, "Let loose the dogs of war ..."

"... and cry havoc."

19

INSTITUTE, WV

THE GLOW from the emergency lighting was all they had as they scoured the rooms for weapons on the security deck and loaded up. Everyone was in a zombie suit. Automatic pistols were strapped on every hip, while the black synthetic .12 gauge shotguns were charged. Myrtle seemed calm as she put two belts of ammunition over the top of Rod's massive shoulders. The big man had a fiery look in his eye as he talked on his short wave radio.

"Status report all stations!" he ordered.

"One check."

"Two check."

"Listen up, this is Command One. We have a breach. Zimmerman 23. Zimmerman 23. Over."

"Check."

"What's Zimmerman 23, over?"

"Zombies are on the loose, fellas. Maybe a dozen. But they're fast. We already have men down. Take the high ground. Report any sightings immediately."

"Roger that."

"Roger."

"Henry, we have four guys out there. The gate's not reporting. What's the plan?"

Everything in the security manual depended on the availability of backup power. The zombie panic room on their floor was locked. The computer stations were dead.

"What do we do, Henry?" Tori was shivering at his side.

He had already seen what the zombies had done to a well-armed security fire team, and he didn't have any inclination to take them on. The last thing he wanted to do was put any more lives in jeopardy. They were either going to have to fight, or hide and hope that the cavalry came in time, but deep inside he didn't figure that was going to happen. He had to give his friends hope even though he didn't have any. He was too smart to figure this for some kind of accident.

I can't believe they're doing this again. WHS playing games with men's lives. They must figure we're worthless or that I know too much.

It seemed that the WHS had other plans for the XT serum. The zombies were moving so fast, and the only thing he could think of was that the serum must be a part of that. No, they weren't trying to cure the zombies; they were trying to control them. All he could figure was that his usefulness must have come to an end. *Burn off the loose ends.* It infuriated him. *Lab rats again.*

"Henry! What do we do?" she said again.

"I'm thinking. Just give me a second."

"Team One to Command One, we've got movement over near your building."

"What've you got?" Rod said.

The man's voice on the radio was almost inaudible.

"Take a look out of your east entrance windows."

"Oh my!" Myrtle cried. "There must be twenty of them coming our way. Geez! They move as fast as us!"

Henry tried to remain calm, but the sight of the zombies swarming the building uncoiled his nerves. He counted the heads bobbing through the fog and was relieved that there weren't any more than ten of them.

Weege shouted, "Shoot them before they get here. Shoot them now!"

"Shut up, Idiot," Tori said. "They don't need to hear us, too."

"They can't hear," Weege said.

"We don't know that, so keep it down for now," said Henry.

"What's your location, Team One? Why aren't you in a secure location?" Rod said.

"Sorry Rod, but the nearest bunker was locked down. We've been all over as far as we could stand to go. We're on top of the Municipal Building now. We can't see in your windows, but we're on the ledge facing you. We had a clean shot on them earlier, but not much that a pistol or shotgun can do from this distance."

"Keep it quiet, watch your back, and let me know if you see anything else. Team Two Report."

"We're good. The bunker in the south quadrant is locked up. The fence is hotter than the 4th of July. No zombies though. Over."

Blam! Blam! Blam!

Everyone lurched. The sound of the shots was muffled and distant.

"Disregard! We've got three walkers! Fast ones!"

Another procession of gunfire rang out from deep in the complex.

"Get on the buildings, Team Two! Shoot at their legs!"

"We're on the building! Damn things keep moving! Got on some kind of suit, like ours. Who in the hell put the walkers in zombie suits!" Rod's face was dripping with sweat, but Henry thought he was handling the situation quite well.

"You should be safe on the building. Hold your fire and save your ammo until help arrives."

"Rod ..."

"What is it?"

"They can climb."

Henry felt the goosebumps rise on his arms. He'd known in the back of his mind that if the zombies were on the XT Formula that it was a possibility. Now, it was confirmed that the zombies were on the formula, and the evil powers of the WHS were at work again. He grabbed Rod by the arm and said, "Tell them to get as close a shot as they can of the zombie's face. It's the best chance.

"Fire Team Two, aim for the face. Over."

He could see the small flashes of light reflecting off the windows in the distance. The steady popping of gunfire gave him hope that the creatures were about to be stopped. Every face in the room was almost pressed against the window as each critical second passed. Then the silence fell. They all looked at each other then back over to Rod, who held the radio up to his lips.

"Fire Team Two, Over."

Nothing.

"Fire Team Two, Over."

"Rod, it's over."

A collective sigh of relief filled the room along with a few fists pumping in the air.

"They didn't make it. We can see the entire thing. One zombie down. Sorry Rod, but they're gone. Fire Team One. Over."

"Dammit!" Rod said. "Those fiends! I must have heard over fifty shots fired, and they're still moving!

We're gonna need some more fire power, Henry! My men ain't gonna die for nothing."

"Hey, what's going on?"

It was Rudy.

"Why are you guys geared up?"

"Tori, get a med kit and give him an oxygen shot."

"Zombies, Rudy. Remember the zombies before you passed out? Well, they're everywhere. Do you know anything about that? Because anything you might know might save all of our lives." He waved his hand across the people in the room. Rudy blanched. "You know something, don't you?"

Tori handed Rudy the oxygen tank and mask. He breathed heavy breaths in and out as his eyes flitted from one face to another. Rudy knew something. Henry was sure of it. Rudy began to stare at Tori's chest as he sucked more into the mask. Henry stepped into his view.

"Rudy, what do you know?"

"I overheard Alice talking to the director about a drill and new zombies. That's all."

"Henry, get over here." Rod was talking from somewhere down the hall. "We've got movement down there."

"Get Rudy in a suit, Myrtle."

He headed down the hall with Tori sticking to his side. Rod had the fire exit door cracked open. The big man said, "Listen."

The voices were haunting and fast.

"Numma-Numma. Numma-Numma."

Tori shrieked. He ran over to the other door and cracked it open.

"Numma-Numma. Numma-Numma."

"They're in both stair wells. Let's get these doors secured."

"We can't lock them without power!" Rod shouted. "We need padlocks and chains!"Rudy had wandered into the hall with his suit half on.

"What's going on?"

"Can you hear that?" Rod said as he charged his shotgun.

The steady sound of Numma-Numma was getting louder in the stairwells.

Rudy looked like he was about to puke when he said, "Yeah."

Rod smiled as he said, "Then grab a weapon, Rudy. The Zombies are coming!"

20

LOCATION UNKNOWN

"YEAH, that creep called me every day for years," Nate said.

Rose, Walker, and Doctor Z all looked at one another. It made him uncomfortable. Who was Harry? The man had been like a steady drip of water: calling, calling, and calling. It was never at the same time of day, either, but rather anytime of the day or night. It was odd to feel either hatred or resentment for someone that he had never met. Harry's calls and voice had even awakened him from his sleep. Countless nights he had lain restless in the bed if Harry hadn't called yet.

Doctor Z stood up and asked, "Have you ever met the man?"

"No."

"Do you think you would recognize him if you saw him?"

It was odd, but for some reason he thought that he would. For years he'd had an image in his mind of what Harry looked like, but for all he knew he had probably met the man a dozen times and didn't know it.

"I doubt it."

The doctor's eyes and voice were probing.

"What if you heard him?"

Nate scratched the back of his neck.

"Well, maybe. At least I think I would, but there were many days when I was pretty sure the person I was talking to wasn't him. It was like him, but different. I always figured it was either his mood or it was a voice box of some kind. Still, it was spooky. The man knew everywhere I had been, and then he'd joke about it with me on the phone."

"How so?"

"Oh, I'd be at a bar and he'd call me at the bar and ask me if I was enjoying my martini. Stuff like that. He was like a ghost or something."

"Someone was watching you, but you were just too stupid to notice," Walker said in his matter-of-fact tone.

"Thanks." He directed his attention back to the doctor. "So, why the interest in Harry?"

Doctor Z was staring into space.

Agitated, Nate snapped his fingers in the man's face.

"Hello! What's the deal with Harry?"

The doctor's phone buzzed in his pocket. His eyebrows perched as he read the message.

"Walker, you and Rose finish this up. I've got another patient."

Nate heard the door shut before he even realized the man had left the room.

"Man, he's a strange one. So where were we?"

Rose took the doctor's place at his bed and said, "Our insiders have been gathering information on Harry for the past several months. They are being led to believe that Harry is the man in charge of the WHS. They think he's the brains behind World Population Control."

"Yes, but why would he be calling me?"

"Because you're the man that foiled his plans. You're the man who can foil them again."

"I just love the insanity of all this, but please continue."

"Think about it: every time you went to a WHS function there were always a bunch of lackeys all around, weren't there?" Rose motioned with her hands. "They were jawing back and forth and talking about all the good they were going to do for the world. Remember all of that?"

Did he ever. It had been fun the first few months,

but it hadn't taken long before he'd been completely sick of it all.

"Sure I remember. They were all so smug and insincere. Liars, every last one of them."

"If you had to think about it, would any of them make you think of Harry?"

"No. I mean, I really never hit if off of any of them. I'd recognize some faces and names, but they all would have been all over the papers, too."

"Sometimes Nate, the best place to hide is in plain sight."

"Especially when you have a new face," Walker chuckled.

"What are you saying? I can't go around those people."

Rose nodded over at Walker and said, "Let me show you something."

Walker grabbed a computer and handed it over. She turned the display his way.

"Do any of them look familiar?" she asked.

It was a group photo taken at WHS headquarters in Washington DC. Nate was in the picture surrounded by nine other smiling people. Six men and Three women. One just as disingenuous as the next.

"I know them all by name. Do you think one of them is Harry?"

"Maybe. This picture was taken years ago, and at this point in time we know that this group is the highest authority in the WHS. Harry could be one of them, or one of them might know who Harry is. What do you think about this guy?"

She tapped the screen, and a larger picture of an older and distinguished man popped up.

"That's Don Baker." He sucked the rest of his Mountain Dew out with a straw. "He wasn't so bad; he knew some good jokes, at least. But, he seems too old to have been Harry."

"How about her?"

"What is this, a line up? Look, if they're all so bad, why don't you just go send Walker in to kill them all?"

Walker smiled and said, "That's what I said. I think that Taco Bell's making him smarter, Rose."

She shook her head.

"It's been discussed, but the security is too heavy. You know that. But, if we can find the right one and take a shot, we think we can take down the rest of them."

"So you want to cut the head off the snake, huh?"

"No, more like a dragon."

"Then you better hope it only has one head. So what do you want me to do?"

"We're going to reunite you with your old friends. Just get you in the same room. Walker's got it all set up."

"What?" Henry felt his food start to come back up. "I'm not a spy. And they're looking for me? No way, I'm not doing that. Can't you just get me a video or something?"

"We've tried." Rose grabbed his hand and squeezed it. "Nate, the next outbreak is coming soon. We don't have much time. We've run into a bunch of dead ends. As of now, you're Plan C. We are sorry to ask, Nate, but the world needs you again."

Her soft red lips were convincing, and her pretty eyes were pleading. How could he possibly say no?

"Okay," he gave in, "but I have one request before you send me to my next death."

"What is it, Honey?"

He whispered something in her ear.

Rose smiled at Walker and said, "I'll take it from here."

Walker grumbled as he shook his head and left the room.

As soon as the door clicked shut, her lips and his were one.

21

Institute, WV

WHAM!

Tori screamed. Henry stepped in front of her. He could hear the unceasing chorus of the zombies: ravenous and violent. It was only a matter of time before they made their way through the doors, unless they broke them down first. He cringed at the thought. The zombies were strong enough, but with the XT Serum they would be even stronger than before.

"Fire Team One to Command. What's your status?"

Horrified, Rudy grabbed Rod's radio and screamed, "We're going to die! Get over here! Get over here now! That's an order!"

Whap.

Rod slapped the man and took back his radio.

"We need a way out of here. Any suggestions?"

WHAM!

WHAM!

WHAM!

"Try the fire escapes. We'll give you cover. It's all clear on our side. Over."

Rudy knocked down Weege as he bolted from the group.

Henry yelled after him, "Rudy! Stay with the group!"

As the man's bushy head disappeared down the hall, Henry had a sinking feeling. Everyone's eyes fell to him. Myrtle was picking Weege's shaking form up from the floor. They followed him over and looked down the hall on the opposite end of the main entrance. Rod and Myrtle were standing their ground, shotgun barrels leveled toward the sound of the hungry zombies on the other side of the doors. Everyone's expression was filled with fear.

He heard the door groan somewhere near the elevator's foyer. He expected the zombies to pour through at any second.

"DAMMIT! DAMMIT!" Rudy was yelling, running back down the corridor. "We're trapped. It's sealed! The fire doors are sealed! We're gonna die, Henry! Do something!"

He was afraid of that. The magnetic locks were engaged, making sure nobody was getting in or out. It was his biggest fear. Just like his brother Jimmy, someone, somewhere was calling the shots. He searched for the cameras near the ceilings and noticed a tiny red light burning on the top of each and every one. Some-one, somewhere was watching. *Bastards!* But he couldn't say a word. Despair filled him from his chin to his knees.

"Henry," Tori grabbed his face, "Henry, don't you give up. Turn on that brain of yours, and get us out of here. We need you, Henry! I need you. I don't want to die like this!"

At that moment, the pounding stopped, but the moans and the numma-nummas remained. Henry was so sick of that sound that his despair began to melt away and harden like iron.

"Everyone, get your masks on. Just because we don't have a door doesn't mean we can't take the window."

"What! We're three stories up! I ain't jumping. I hate heights," Rod said.

WHAM!

"Look, I'll cover you crazy people, but I'm not jumping out some window."

"I'm with you," Myrtle added. The short woman looked and walked like an Ewok in her zombie suit.

"Let me have your radio, Rod," he said. "Fire Team One, this is Henry. We're gonna have to make our own door. Do we have anything below us to jump on?"

"You've got to say over, Dude?" Rudy slurred.

"Shut up!" Weege said, slapping Rudy in the head. "And put your mask on!"

"Everyone be quiet! Shush!" Myrtle said. "Do you hear that?"

Their necks all tilted. He could hear the sound of the metal doors groaning and popping. The moaning became louder with every creaking sound.

"There's a utility building about 5 feet out from the wing. The jump doesn't look so bad. Better than being zombie chow anyway. Over."

Henry rushed over to the window as the zombies filled the hallway. *Where's that utility building?* The windows were large panes of heavy glass that didn't open or close.

Numma-numma.

Boom! Boom!

A symphony of thunder had entered the room.

Henry's head whipped around just in time to see the first wave of the invading hoard. Four zombies were charging into the room on stiff legs. Rod's and Myrtle's shotguns rang out and knocked a zombie backward onto the floor.

"Get us out of here, Henry!" shouted Rod. "They're getting back up!"

"Reload!" Myrtle shouted, handing the man more shells.

The zombie lurched back up, mouth clutching open and shut. The metal mask seemed to restore a small portion of its humanity, but its intent seemed more deadly.

Henry lowered his shotgun and blasted out the window. He jumped up on top of the desk alongside the window ledge and shouted for Tori.

"Come on!" She reached out, and he pulled her up. She clutched at his chest as she looked over his shoulder. The sound of the shotgun blasts was deafening, and she was shaking her head.

"You've got to jump!"

"I can't! It's too high."

Weege and Rudy were at his side.

Weege looked outside and said, "Just hang over the ledge — like this!" The little man tossed his shotgun out the window and swung his body over the ledge. "The glass can't cut you through the suit!" he yelled, clutching the jagged edge of the window with his gloved fingertips. "Come on, I'll catch you. Better this than being zombie food!" He dropped down, landed on his feet, and fell flat on his back. "See!"

BLAM! BLAM! BLAM!

Rod was shouting.

"GET MOVING, HENRY! We can't reload fast enough! Damn things keep coming!"

Henry grabbed Tori and lowered her to the ledge.

"Hurry up, Dude!" Rudy screamed as he forced himself to the ledge.

Somebody was screaming. Henry looked over his shoulder and saw Myrtle's squat figure ramming the stock of her gun into the face of a zombie. Behind the fray, more zombies were coming.

"LET GO, TORI!" He shouted, rushing to Myrtle's aid, shotgun blasting at everything moving his way.

"Get out of here, Henry!" Rod shoved him back. "I got this!"

Myrtle was pinned under two zombies now, each tearing at her suit. He saw the woman stuff a pistol in one of the creature's mouths and fire away. It slumped over as another bit into her arm. Rod opened up a barrage into the creature's back. Another half dozen zombies were closing in. Some were crawling from the impact of their wounds, but they still came. Myrtle screamed a curse at the zombies, then she screamed no more. Henry felt sick.

"Henry, go! Take care of the others!"

He looked back at the widow, and Tori and Rudy were gone. Rod was the only thing between him and the zombies tearing him to shreds. The big man looked like a super hero in his suit as he fired into the zombies. Henry's fear consumed him as he backpedaled to the window. He could hear Tori screaming for him from down below. He took one last glance at Rod—the bravest man he ever saw—mumbled a prayer, and jumped.

22

Washington, DC

"So ... Do you have your checkbook with you, Uncle Don?" Jack asked in a mocking tone.

Don laughed. It was a better than revealing what he really wanted to do to his demented nephew. He cleared his throat.

"Don't you worry about the money, Jack. I've got plenty of that."

"I don't suppose you want to increase your wager then, double or nothing?"

Even though Don's stomach was recoiling inside him, he was still enthralled with what he was watching. The zombie vision was much more effective than he ever would have imagined. The views kept changing in order to keep their eyes closer to the action. It reminded him of all the camera angles in sports that seemed to be everywhere at once. The picture on his screen went from one zombie point of view to another, and he couldn't help but wonder what the other people behind all of this were thinking. Were they just as sadistic as his nephew had become?

"I think we can leave things as they are, Jack. I'm not as willing to part with my money as you might be, especially when the deck is stacked against me."

"Okay then." Jack typed a few more commands on his screen. "Watch these things go! They are so relentless."

The zombies had made their way into a stairwell and began pounding at the doors that barred their path. Don still had the sound muted on his machine, but he could hear the zombies pounding and moaning on Jack's.

"Watch this. I'm going to try and get this zombie to open the door. They just need to push that thumb lever down on the handle. Ah, it's not working. They're all too bunched together."

"Won't the people inside just take the fire escape?"

"All of the perimeter doors are sealed."

"Can't you open the interior doors?"

"No. Just good old fashioned fire doors. The kind your generation probably made by hand." Jack chuckled. "The main goal was to keep zombies from getting in or out."

Years ago, Don had plenty of relatives, many of

which he hadn't spent much time with, but they had all been amiable folk. Up until today, Jack had been one of his favorites, but the young man's callous behavior had him making mental alterations to his will. *This has got to be stopped.* What could he do, though? His nephew was just executing orders, and he would be obligated to do the same if he was given those same orders. There would be a difference had he been given the same charge though. He wouldn't be enjoying it.

He was holding his screen in both hands when the zombies made their push through.

"Yes!" Jack exclaimed.

Damn! Don had already watched two of the three remaining security fire teams fall into the clutches of the charged-up zombies. He was certain he would have nightmares for the rest of his life after this. It was like watching a horror movie from the monster's point of view.

The sounds of screaming voices and cracks of gunfire now filled the air, along with the sounds of the moaning zombies. Don felt a sliver of hope when he noticed that the men and women in the room were clad in full zombie suits and were fully armed for battle. The image on his screen shook and tumbled downward, only to be switched over to another point of view a moment later. A man had blasted out a window, drawing a curse from his nephew's lips. *Yes!*

"Ah, don't get too excited, Uncle. They won't be going anywhere on broken legs."

"Maybe so, but the sunrise is still getting closer."

"Huh ..."

A stumpy figure in a zombie suit stuffed a pistol in a zombie's face and fired. Don and Jack dropped their screens as they both jumped from their seats. Don's heart was pounding inside his chest as Oliver made his way over to help him back on the bench.

"You okay, Sir?"

Don looked up into the man's stone face and felt relief. Oliver reminded him he was still a part of humanity. He said, "Thanks, Oliver, I'm okay. Whew!"

Oliver handed him a handkerchief. "You're sweating, Sir."

Jack was back in his seat, laughing. "That was awesome! Hey Oliver, you need to go. You can't see this. I'll take care of Uncle Don. You just keep his coffee warm. It'll be over soon."

Don didn't like the condescending tone in his nephew's voice.

"Oliver works for me, not you, Jack. Mind your tongue."

"Yeah, whatever ..."

"I'm alright, Oliver. Best you go."

Oliver frowned as he glanced over at Jack before he walked away.

"I hope you don't treat most people that way," Don said.

Jack didn't respond, his face was intent on his screen.

Don picked his computer up with a sigh. Two more figures were no longer in the room he viewed, leaving only two standing. One was a large man, he figured, based off the view he had of the zombies looking up. A shotgun was blasting into all of them. He heard the large man yell, "Henry, go! Take care of the others!"

Ah … Henry Bawkula lives. A thrill went through him. He knew enough about Henry to know that he was a capable man. Don had seen all the footage from what happened at WHS Facility III, the Zombie Day Care. *I wonder if he's still with that Italian girl who lost her arm. She was something.* The big man in the room was holding off the zombies when Henry jumped from the window. The butt of a rifle slammed into his screen, causing his finger tips to tingle. The view was gone.

"Dammit!" Jack cried, shaking his screen like an angry child.

Don chuckled. "Time's ticking."

Another view popped up that was closing in on the big man tossing away his shotgun and reaching for another. Jack was pounding his hand into his screen. "I think we lost sound. Damn. I wanted hear this big man scream!"

Don felt a chill as he watched the throng of zombies rush after the man.

23

INSTITUTE, WV

ROD. He had been known as one of the biggest and baddest fighters on the Eastern Seaboard. For over 15 years he had fought in anything from a cage to a parking lot. Never once had he shown fear or shed a tear. He'd been known as the Black Python in the Octagon. He'd kicked like a mule and punched like a heavy weight. He was big, fast, fluid, and feared. He'd had that advantage over his opponents because they were living. This fight was different. His adversaries were dead.

He let off his last round, imploding the face of his latest attacker. It sagged to the ground as another stiff creature took its place, arms clutching at his neck. Two automatic pistols were blazing in his hands. The bullets punched into the bodies of the undead, slowing them a tad. *Head shot! Head shot! Head shot!* The rounds ricocheted from the metal foreheads as the relentless gang surged forward. Rod dove behind a counter and reloaded.

BLAM!

He caught one in the knee, sending it reeling to the ground.

"Yeah baby!"

Ka-Blam! Ka-Blam!

Two more dropped, but they were still crawling. The others were closing in from all directions.

He glanced at the window. Henry was gone. *I've got to get out of here!*

"Ugh!"

Something heavy slammed into him. The stench of the dead filled his nostrils. He fired a series of rounds over his shoulder, every bullet lethal. No effect. A zombie was biting into his suit, and another was pulling him down.

"NO!"

Fear assailed him. If bullets couldn't stop his enemies, then what would?

"NO!"

Rod wasn't going to die like this. He was the Black Python.

"NO!" He flipped the zombie from his back.

Octagon Legend.

"NO!" His boot crushed another's jaw.

As anger coursed through his big body so did the adrenaline. He had started fighting when he was ten. 25 years of training hadn't prepared him for a day like this ... but it would have to do.

The zombies were fast. The zombies were strong ... unyielding. But, the zombies couldn't fight worth a shit.

"Come on, you dead bastards!"

A roundhouse kick sent one staggering to the floor.

"You can't touch me!"

Two more crashed into each other as Rod jumped away. Another clutched at his neck. Rod snapped its wrist. He stuffed its fist inside its own mouth and swept its legs from underneath it. The zombies were writhing all around him now as he jumped, dodged, and dived. The zombies were inferior in size, average men, nowhere close to his height or weight. The death match was becoming a mismatch.

"Let go, you—urk!"

He cracked his head as he was pulled to the ground. Warm blood was seeping into his eyes and the hoard went into a frenzy. The mangled mass became a creeping doom. Rod twisted away from the clutches of two disabled zombies and dashed towards the stair-well. Two zombies cut off his path as they closed in.

"Damn!"

His chest was burning now. He scanned around in the dim light, looking for a weapon of any kind. He bolted into the security room, grabbed a chair, and slung it into the zombies. One toppled over. The other came on. Its fingers tried to tear off his mask. Rod snatched the monster up, hurled it into the others, and yelled.

Now one was hanging on his leg, biting into his ankle. It felt like his leg was in a vice. He screamed. Reaching down, he grabbed the back of its head and tore off its mask. He couldn't see much in the darkness, but there was a skull. He ripped his hunting knife from his belt and plunged it into the back of its skull. He pulled it out just in time to thrust it under the chin of another. He lost his grip

"R-Rah!" he bellowed as he tore through the hoard and headed for the window. The zombie suit was the only thing saving him from being ripped to shreds. There must have been four hundred pounds of zombies tearing into him as he fought for every step. The window was only ten feet away. He could hear voices screaming from down below.

"I'M COMING!"

Like wild animals, the zombies clawed at him and bit into his suit. It held, but the skin and muscles underneath were getting torn. Rod's body was on fire, and the pain was blinding. Sweat and blood seeped into his eyes. *NO! I can't die like this!*

The window was only five feet away from his outstretched grasp.

"Gotta! ... Keep! ... Moving!"

He made another step, dragging a zombie like an angry child. He was so close now, but his body didn't have the energy to make another step. Just one more step. *Please Lord, give me the strength.*

FROM DOWN BELOW they all gasped at the sight. Rod's massive frame appeared in the window, clutching at the ledge. Henry shouted helplessly as the zombies covering the man began pulling him back in. The big man held on, his big gloved hands digging into the metal window pane.

"Come on, Rod!"

Henry thought he heard his friend say *'Run'* as he was pulled back into the darkness.

24

LOCATION UNKNOWN

NATE MCDANIEL'S life had been rebooted. New face. New clothes. New Job ... WHS Security Squad. *What a joke.* He scratched his face. His once heavy beard was nice and trim with a touch of gray around the chin. In the mirror he tried making faces. He smiled and frowned. Made an angry face and chuckled at himself. He started to sing.

"Don't talk stupid," Walker said, combing his hair at the mirror by his side.

He still had that at least, the voice. *Smooth as silk and sweeter than honey.* That's what Rose had said after they advanced their relationship several hours ago.

He followed Walker into the parking garage out of the strange building that he assumed had been his home for the past several months. His legs and face ached from the effort. Walking down the stairs winded him. He got into the passenger side of a slate gray sedan with a WHS logo on the side. The moment of eeriness passed as they pulled out of the garage and headed down the road. He thought about Rose's sweet lips the entire car ride over. He still didn't know where he left from for sure, but it wasn't long before he knew exactly where he was. It was a place he had become quite fond of over the years: Washington, DC. Head-quarters of the WHS and this year's host of their Zombie Convention.

"Stay close to me. You've got all of the ID and credentials that you need. If someone says something to you, just nod or shake your head. Security is tight here."

Nate wiped his sweaty hands on his pants and said in a gruff voice, "Okay."

"Geez, that's bad. You sound like the Hulk. But, I guess it will do."

"Nate smash Walker," Nate said, imitating the Incredible Hulk.

"Shad-dup."

He rolled down his window and inhaled. The cool air was refreshing. The lights of the city and the nation's Capitol were captivating. He loved it here. Of course, the WHS hadn't given him much choice. Even if he could live somewhere else, he wasn't so certain that he would. The exhilarating feeling of freedom and a new life was soon dimmed as an image of Christy Backwater was etched in his head. She had been gorgeous, seductive, and powerful. He could still feel her sticky blood on his hands. He rubbed his fingertips together. *I can't believe she was going to kill me.* He coughed.

"I'm not putting my cigarette out, if that's what you're hinting at," Walker said.

"Huh ... no, I couldn't care less. As a matter of fact, I wouldn't mind one, myself."

"Is that so? Well, help yourself. Glove box."

He grabbed a box of Camel non-filters.

"They still make these things?"

"In some states."

The smoke burned his lungs as he inhaled. He sighed with a heavy breath of smoke.

"Rose isn't gonna like that. Doctor Z, either."

"I guess they can transplant new lungs to go with my new face, then."

"Yeah, good one."

Solid country gold songs were playing on the radio as Nate watched the street signs he passed by. The music wasn't as offensive as he used to think, more soothing than anything. He didn't figure he should expect much better from a skinny hick like Walker anyway. After a few more songs played and his second cigarette was extinguished, he figured he needed a better idea of what he was getting into.

"Walker ..."

The man came to a stop at a light and said, "I know what you're thinking. What are you going to do when we get there?"

"Well yeah ... What am I going to do when I get there?"

"Follow me. Stay close. Do as I do and say. We're going to be among your old comrades of the WHS. Watch. Listen. Maybe we'll learn something."

It didn't make any sense to him. They wouldn't say anything in front of them. He knew them well enough to know that when they had something important on their minds they would dismiss themselves. Never once did they keep him around for the more important plans. He had tried several times to include himself, but he'd usually been met with a courteous "No."

"I'm not a spy. I'm just some dude that got lucky, is all," he confessed. "You know that, of course, and I'm sure you resent that."

The car was moving again.

"I know that ... but ... man I hate to say this ... the truth is, I believe that everybody is somebody. Even an over-glamorized fornicator like you."

"Hey!"

"Heh-heh. You know it's true. Besides, I'd be lying if I said I wasn't' just like all the other men in the world that wanted to be you just for a day. The star of the century."

"It's a joke."

"Maybe so, but you have a purpose. You stopped

the zombies once. You can stop them again. It's probably why you are here."

"Great. So, why are you here, then? Have you figured it out yet?"

"I'm pretty sure I'm here to kill zombies." Walker lit up another cigarette. "And the people that make zombies."

"Sounds pretty simple. I save the world. You kill the zombies. Maybe we should come up with a name for ourselves," Nate suggested.

"Well, the Dynamic Duo is taken. So is the Green Hornet and Kato."

"Hawkman and smoking Hawkman."

"Creampuff and Studman."

"Milk and Honey."

"Better yet, Big Guy and Little Guy."

"The Undertaker ..."

"... and Kane." Nate finished. "I don't even have a real name now, do I?"

Walker tossed him a thin wallet. Inside, there was an I.D. without a picture on it. It had a name, though.

"Rick Jones. Seriously."

"It's all that I could think of. I'm not exactly good with names."

It wasn't so bad. After all, Rick Jones was a hero of sorts. If not for him, there never would have been an Incredible Hulk. The tension between the two men had subsided. Even Walker's stiff talk had loosened up.

The man's dry sense of humor had begun to grow on him.

"Nah, it's good. It's not as cool as Bruce Banner, but it's still better than Clark Kent."

"True. I almost used Chuck Jones."

Nate's brows perched as he nodded. He pulled down his vanity mirror and said, "I can see that, too."

Men could easily find common ground with one another if they were willing to speak. Sports, comic books, movies, and video games were all part of their mental playground. The doubt inside his belly about the skinny man in black began to subside. Maybe Walker was on his side. Maybe it wasn't all a hoax. *Keep playing along.*

"We're almost to the convention center. WHS security is going to check you in. Show your ID. They scan it and your face."

"My face?"

"Don't worry. You've already been added into the database. Worst case scenario, we head back to the car ... or die."

"What?"

Walker showed him a thin-lipped smile as they pulled into the garage and said, "It'll be okay. Besides, you've already died once."

25

INSTITUTE, WV

"HENRY! HENRY!"

Someone was screaming as he gawped at the window above.

"Get down here!"

He didn't want to move, but someone was pulling him away. He resisted.

"He's gone, Henry! Come on, Lover, we've got to move on!" Tori said, tears streaming from her eyes.

They both limped towards the ladder. Tori grunted with every step.

"You okay?"

"Just my ankle.

THUMP!

A zombie dropped from the window and crashed on top of the roof.

THUMP!

Another followed.

"Get down, Tori!" he said, looking down the ladder. Rudy and Weege were down below, shouting at him.

"BAWK! COME ON!" Rudy cried.

He spotted two 4-seater utility vehicles and Security Team One. They were all waving him on. The moans behind him became even louder as one zombie rose to its feet in pursuit.

"GERONIMO!"

One of the biggest men he ever knew was jumping from the window. A sickening crunch followed as Rod landed on top of the zombie. Henry rushed over and pulled the man up from the ground. The other zombie was crawling, dragging its busted legs behind it. Henry kicked away its outstretched hand. As the pair of men stumbled to the ladder, the zombies began jumping from the windows like the building was on fire. Henry watched in awe as Rod slid down on the outer rails of the fire escape.

"MOVE, HENRY!"

Rod caught him as he leaped down the last ten feet. "OW!"

"You'll be okay," Rod said, dragging him towards the awaiting vehicles.

"Thank God you're alive!" Henry exclaimed.

Rod didn't reply as he looked upward. Tori, Weege

and Rudy were screaming. The zombies were scrambling off the top of the roof.

Rod shouted, "Get us out of here, Doug!!"

"Where? There's nowhere to go!"

"Just go! We'll think of something on the way."

The Gators sped off.

Doug, Henry, Rod, and another security member were in one Gator. The Weege, Rudy, and Tori were being driven by another member. Everyone had pulled the mesh masks up from their faces. Henry almost enjoyed the cold air on his as they sped through the thick fog.

The complex had the feeling of a haunted village now. The contours of the buildings were distorted, and the blacktopped roads were hidden. All of the lamp-posts that littered the compound were dark, and most of the emergency lights were dim. Henry tapped Doug the driver on the shoulder.

"Stop. Let's regroup."

The other Gator pulled along their side. Every face was wide-eyed with horror. They were beside a small chapel that was covered in ivy. A small cemetery was nearby. Rudy retched over the side of the ATV as Tori climbed over into the seat beside Henry. Everyone was looking back and forth at one another with heads craning for any sounds of pursuit.

Weege was the first to speak.

"We have to find the director and Alice, Henry. They'll know what to do. Let's go to his quadrant."

Doug was loading shells into his shotgun as he said, "Nope. We checked, or at least the other guys did. They're either sealed up somewhere or on the run. Probably dead."

It didn't seem likely to Henry. Alice had to have been in on something. His gut told him that much. With so many personnel at the Zombie Conference, it didn't seem likely that they'd leave the director behind, unless they wanted him gone as well. As for Alice, she was too much of a suck-up to be black listed. If anyone knew what was going on, he was certain that she would. In the meantime, he had to find a way out of this trap.

"Anybody have any ideas?" he said, looking around.

"More ammo. We couldn't check the munitions depot. They might have heavier stuff in there," one security man said.

"Some armor-piercing rounds would be nice. It's the only thing that'll bust through those metal skulls. Man! What's going on here, Henry? Somebody let those zombies loose ... didn't they?" Rod said, letting out a painful groan.

"You okay?" Tori asked.

"I'm torn up. Busted bones." Rod pulled off his mask and spit blood. "I'm still a man, though."

Henry put his hand on the man's shoulder and said, "Rod ... everyone ... I can't say what's going on, but it looks like the WHS is up to its dirty tricks."

"What do you mean?" one guard asked.

"Without getting into detail, I have knowledge of experiments of theirs. There's a formula that was supposed to cure the zombies, but instead it just sped them up. They were testing it on children, but now they've moved on to adults. I think they are making zombie soldiers." He ran his fingers back through his hair. "And their first war is with us. A bunch of nobodies. Casualties of the greater good, I'd assume."

There was silence. Only the chirping of nature's creatures remained. Henry felt like he had sucked the hope from each and every one of them. Every face was sweaty and drained. Even his own hands were trembling. He started to continue, but Rod's powerful voice cut him off.

"I'm not dying for nothing. I'm not a victim. If it's a fight they want, it's a fight I'll give them." The man was looking at the cross on the roof of the small church. Rod groaned as he left the Gator and said, "Everybody gather around ... I want to say something."

Henry thought he knew what the man was doing, but he didn't think the others would respond. They all gathered in.

"Everyone hold hands and bow your heads."

Henry grabbed Weege on his left and Tori on his right. The small circle was complete. He glanced up at the old metal cross that was illuminated in the pale moonlight.

Rod said, "God ... please help us get the hell out of here alive. Amen."

A few others mumbled the final word as well.

"Henry. Henry," Weege was squeezing his hand.

"Yeah."

The little man's eyes were feverish with excitement.

"I have an idea."

"I'm all ears."

So was everyone else.

"We need blood. Lots of blood."

"What for? We—"

"Ssssh!" Tori said. "Do you hear that?"

The sound was very distinct.

"Numma-numma. Numma-numma ..".

And getting louder.

"Get back in the Gators!"

"Henry, listen to me! Let's head for the gym! I have an idea. We have to get blood!"

Not a second after they started moving, the zombies erupted from the fog like rabid dogs.

"GO!"

The zombies were blocking their path.

26

Washington, DC

Now, Don was the one laughing. His nephew Jack was cursing at his custom laptop.

"Impossible!"

Don swore that if that big man in the zombie suit survived, he would put him directly on his payroll and hope the man never learned he had been an associate in his attempted death. At this point, Don was titillated. The massive man slung the zombies around like rag dolls. The WHS team that worked the cameras must have been having a fit. His screen went black on several occasions, only to emerge again with another pummeling scene. He swore he felt his jaws rattle a couple of times.

"Don't get cocky, Uncle. See, the man's out of energy, and the zombies have just begun."

It was a hard thing, watching the valiant man begin to die. The swarm covered the fighter. The screen didn't pick up much of the picture, but it was pretty clear this battle was over. Don's heart was heavy for a moment, and then something amazing happened. His view of the screen changed, and suddenly he was sailing through the air and crashing on top of a gravel roof. After the camera switched, the big man was on the lower roof and hustling over the side. Henry Bawkula was there, too.

"Yes!"

Jack sneered.

"That was just luck. Those people don't have anywhere to run. No escape, and they are running out of ammo."

"True, but it's still getting closer to the dawn. Let me ask you something, Jack. Have you ever taken a moment to ever consider what it might be like if you were in there?"

"No. The only thing that matters is that I'm not in there."

"Suppose that was you. Do you think you could survive? After all, you're smarter than the zombies. What would you do?"

Don waited for the reply, but the only response was the man's fingers moving feverishly over his keyboard.

"Well ... I guess I'll assume you would give up and die, then."

"I'd think of something."

"Ah ... so, don't you think they'll think of something, as well?"

Jack threw his arms out in front of himself and said, "I don't care what they think. It won't matter. They won't survive. No one has, so far."

Wow! Don couldn't help but worry about his status with the WHS. His nephew, someone that he had brought up within that organization, was now privy to information that he was not. His stomach soured as he ran his hand over his face. He became very cold.

Jack continued his gloating.

"How much do you really know about the zombies anyway, Don?"

It was an insult. He knew as much about zombies as anybody. What he knew about the functions of the XT Serum was another matter. Still, the question pissed him off.

"Here's what I know. They are a virus. Man made. An abomination. Something that happens, I believe, when man is saturated by evil. Mindless and hungry with an appetite that cannot be satisfied. And like any other virus, they attack. Infect. Cells and flesh. In this more extreme case, the zombies are hunting blood. They want to infect it. Everyone thinks they are flesh eaters—like cannibals—but if that were the case we wouldn't have any zombies. They would all consume themselves.

"Although I've always enjoyed the headlines ... ZOMBIE EATS MAN'S BRAIN, all of that is bunk. Do you know how much pressure it would take to crack a human skull? How can a man bite into another man's head? Our teeth aren't designed to be can openers. If a zombie ever ate a brain, it was only because it had already been spilled. Besides, what's the best way to kill a zombie? Pierce the brain. Why would a virus kill itself? No brains, no zombies."

Jack was nodding.

"True. But you've got to love all of those old movies. I bet your generation never saw that becoming real."

"We didn't expect to land on the moon, either. Or have a bomb that could destroy an entire country."

"Well, it looks like every generation has its achievements, some good and some bad. Real bad. Still, Uncle, I don't think you are telling me everything you know about the zombies. The 101 segment doesn't help. Can't you at least tell me where they came from? Who created the virus? About the first outbreak?"

Don didn't like the intensity in Jack's voice. For a moment, his nephew looked like a man obsessed with something dark. He looked Jack in the eyes and said, "You seem to already know enough, Jack. You know things that I don't even know. You're doing things that I wouldn't even consider. And now, you want me to share with you everything that I know?" He cleared his throat. "I do what I do because I have to. That doesn't mean that I enjoy it. Look at you. People are dying, and you like it. Don't you?"

Jack tore his eyes away saying, "No."

"It sure seems like it."

"Can't you just tell me who you think is behind the outbreak?"

"No."

"Do you even know?"

Don paused before he shook his head saying, "No."

Jack hissed through his teeth and returned his interest back to his screen. Don checked his. Only the view of the fog remained. He was relieved.

Good

"Looks like they lost them, and the time's still ticking away."

"They'll sniff them out soon enough."

Don hoped not.

"See look! They're already on the trail."

Don looked down at his screen just in time to see his zombie view getting run over by a Gator full of a bunch of shooting people. As exciting as that was, a troubling feeling remained. He was beginning to get a sinking feeling that he wasn't holding the purse strings anymore. He looked over his shoulder. Oliver was still standing outside the car and smoking. *Am I still in charge here?* Maybe his nephew was ... and he might be in trouble.

27

Institute, **WV**

THEY LIVED. Gators, bullets, zombie suits, and gas propelled the small band of survivors through the latest zombie onslaught. Two zombies were smashed into the payment like roadkill while another got lanced with an 8-foot strip of rebar. No one looked back as they fled through the undead blockade and headed down the road. Now they were stuck, and time was running out. The zombies would be there soon.

Rod and the rest of the security team were slamming the butts of their guns into the gymnasium's door. The magnetic locks weren't giving in.

"Henry, we gotta go! This ain't gonna work," Rod said.

Henry swore he could hear the zombie moans coming.

From behind the wheel of the Gator, Doug shouted, "Get the hell out of the way. I'm making a hole!"

Henry and Tori jumped out of the ATV as the machine barreled toward the heavy metal doors. The sound of bending steel meeting all-wheel drive mayhem crashed into their ears. The Gator plunged inside the darkness.

"Damn. He did it!"

The Gator was still running as they all rushed inside to give thanks to the man. Doug sat unmoving in his seat. A large piece of metal had cut into his head. Henry pulled Tori close as she sobbed.

"Ah man," Rod exclaimed. "I guess it's better dying like this than the other way."

In the distance the moaning became louder.

Weege was yelling, "Come on! Come on! We need the blood. The storage is this way!"

"What the hell is he talking about, Henry?" Tori said. "And I can't see a damn thing!"

A small flashlight beam was glaring in their eyes. It was one of the security team guys. Henry didn't know him.

"Follow you, or follow him?"

"Ow!" Weege screamed from somewhere in the dark.

"Find him," Henry said, "and we'll follow. I think I might know what he's thinking."

"Wherever we're going, let's get there! Those zombies will be here any second," Rod said.

Henry was pulling Tori through the darkness as small beacons of light led the way. Weege was on the gymnasium floor holding his ankle. Rudy stumbled over to the little man and helped him up from the floor.

"What are you doing, you little idiot? What do we want blood for?"

A bright light flashed inside Henry's head. He knew what Weege wanted to do. The zombies wanted blood. The blood bank would give them that.

"Come on, this way everybody," he said, leading the way to a lab room in the back.

Henry knew that the zombie contagion spread through the blood. Testing revealed that living flesh fired the hunting instincts of the zombies, letting them track people for miles. But there was more to it than just the living bodies. There had to be blood inside them as well. Despite what many people figured, brains weren't the object of their ravenous hunger. It was the drive to infect and spread, and only the blood stream could carry that. Still, would stored blood satisfy the zombies' appetites?

Rudy pulled open the door of a walk-in refrigerator and Henry stepped inside. Bags of blood were lit up by the small flashlights.

"What in the world?" Rod gasped. "What's all of this blood for?"

"Transfusions. They try different types to give the zombies new blood. Flush out the corrupted stuff," Weege said.

"Does it work?" Rod asked.

"Er ... testing is inconclusive. Now shut up and grab some bags," Weege ordered.

Rudy began passing them down the line, everyone filling their hands.

"This won't work, you moron. We need to hide," Rudy commented.

"Shut up, you drunkard," Weege fired back. "You hopeless sack of camel dung!"

One of the fire team members spoke up and asked, "What are we supposed to do with it?"

"They'll follow a blood trail," Henry said. "Someone look for a something to carry this stuff in."

"Ssshh!" said a security guard that was watching the door. "I think I hear something."

As everyone shuffled out of the room, all eyes followed the light illuminating the hall. The emergency lights added an additional bit of dim lighting. There was a lot of heavy breathing in the silence and the rattling of weapons being fingered. Henry tried to settle himself down. How many more zombies were out there? How many could they fight off? A dozen bags of blood would only slow them down. They needed a place to hide. But where? *Think Henry! Think.*

"Where to, Henry?" Rod asked.

"Dude, I found some garbage bags," Rudy said. "I've got about ten more pints in here."

"Ssshh!" Tori said.

A distant sound was echoing down the corridor.*"Numma-numma. numma-numma ... "*

Henry set a pint down on the floor and pulled out the Swiss Army knife that his step-father Stanley had given him for his birthday. He cut the bag open and slung it down the hallway.

"What are you doing, Henry? You'll lead them right to us!"

He could feel their confusion. Every stare was of desperation in the dimness.

He was confident when he spoke.

"No, I'm leading them to the pool."

"The pool?" someone said.

Weege said in an excited voice, "That's right, zombies can't swim!"

They left a trail of blood as they dashed through the hallways and burst into the aquatic center. The smell of chlorine was heavy in the gloom. They sliced open a few more bags, set them near the edge of the pool, and waited.

"I'm burning up."

"Let's find a way out of here."

"We're all going to die," Rudy said.

"Shut up!" They all replied.

Henry scanned the room. There were four exits,

and the zombies could burst inside from any one of them. They had come through the door on the east wing, and a there was an opposite one from the west. The north side had two more doors that led back outside, but they were probably locked.

"How are we going to get them in the pool, Henry?" Tori said.

"I guess we're going to have to push them in."

"I'm not doing that!" Weege said.

"Me either!" Rudy agreed.

"We're going to have to make a stand. This is our only chance, unless someone has a better idea?"

Everyone was looking at one another, sweaty and miserable. The heat was unbearable inside the suits and the sweltering building. Henry figured everyone would just as soon die as suffer inside their zombie suits any longer. He was exhausted, too. He checked his weapon. One full clip left. He switched it with the other. Everyone else followed suit except for Weege and Rudy, who were whispering back and forth to each other.

"Rudy, do you care to fill us in?" Henry said.

"Ah ... well, Weege and I have decided that we would rather take our own chances. If you guys want to stay and die by the poolside, that's fine, but we think we can do better on our own."

"Our best chance is to stick together."

"Let them go, Henry," Rod said. "I'm staying."

"There's nowhere to go, unless you know something that you aren't telling us?"

"Good luck, Henry," Weege said as the two men scurried away through the other set of doors.

Henry started to go after him, but Tori held him back. She said, "Those two won't make it very far."

"That's what I'm afraid of."

It was down to him, Tori, Rod, and two security men that he didn't know. Half a dozen zombies would be there any second. Henry knew that they would only get one shot at this, so he had to be sure it worked. They would probably only get one chance. It was time to make a sacrifice.

"Rod, double check those doors over there."

He started to remove his zombie suit.

"What are you doing?" Tori said.

"I'm getting in the water."

"Why?"

"I'm going to draw them in after me, while you guys hide."

Rod yelled over, "These doors won't budge, Henry!"

"You aren't the best swimmer, Henry. Let those guys go."

"No! It's too dangerous. I'll be fine."

Tori stripped down. Henry heard someone gulp in the dark air. She was the perfect figure of sweat and lingerie. Henry grasped after her has she dove into the deep end.

"Ah … it feels so good in here. Sorry, Henry, but I had to get out of that—"

"We've got company, coming fast!" the guard said, backing away and lowering his barrel.

Henry stripped off his suit and dove in alongside Tori. He said, "We'll suffer the madness together."

The moans of the zombies became a roar.

Over half a dozen figures burst inside the aquatic center, smeared with blood. Henry started shouting.

"In here, zombies!"

Tori was whistling and splashing.

The zombies groaned as they piled into one another, fighting over the pints of blood. Two collided at the pool's edge and fell in with a splash. Rod unloaded his shotgun into another, knocking it into the pool.

Henry felt his heart freeze as more zombies spilled through the door.

"This isn't good. Tori, we've got to get out of here."

The blast of weapons rang out like cannons inside the metal dome. A human voice was screaming out in pain. The zombies became a writhing mass of undead flesh as they found the blood and then rushed after the humans in the pool. The pool lights underneath still glowed, and Henry could see the creatures sinking fast under the weight of their metal helmets. He wondered if zombies could drown. Judging by the looks of things, they didn't. They just kept trying to climb up the sides of the pool, so far, in vain.

He and Tori swam towards the shallow end of the pool and hunkered down.

"We've got to make a dash for that door."

Ahead, Rod was backing towards that very door.

"Come on, you two!"

Henry and Tori scrambled out of the pool and dashed for the doors.

BLAM! BLAM! BLAM! click

Henry shoved down the lever of the metal fire doors and surged down the hallway, pulling Tori behind him. Rod was on their heels, and a pack of zombies was on his.

His lungs were bursting inside his chest as he turned down one corridor and into another. He had to make it back outside. Get the Gator and go. He glanced back over his shoulder. Rod was running with a limp, and the zombies were only another twenty feet behind, jaws opened impossibly wide and snapping shut.

"Henry," Tori moaned, "I can't keep up."

"We're almost there. Hang on."

She slipped on a dark streak of something and fell. He pulled her up and hoisted her over his shoulder. Rod was pulling him along now. The zombies had gotten closer. The gymnasium was just ahead, but he knew they wouldn't have enough time to cross it, start the Gator, and run. The zombies would swarm them before they even sat down.

Rod knocked open the next set of fire exit doors. They were back in the gymnasium. So were the two biggest zombies he had ever seen in the world: Rick the Rifle and Slam Dunk Jones. Rod screamed. They looked hungry, and they were coming their way.

Splat! Splat!

Someone was throwing pints of blood at them. Henry twirled around as he stumbled backward with Tori in his arms. Rudy and Weege were heading for the zombie locker that usually housed the giants.

"What are you doing?"

He saw the trash bag filled with pints of blood on the floor. He snatched a pint up. He had an idea. The shadows of the two giants were closing in.

"Rod, throw these at the zombies!"

"What?!"

The zombies in pursuit burst through the door. As if on instinct, Rod hurled the plastic pint of blood into one's mouth. Its jaws clamped down, making a spray of blood. Henry tore the top from another sack and tossed it onto the giant zombies.

"Come on!" he said, running for the zombie locker where Weege and Rudy had begun to close the door. "NOOOO!" he screamed.

The door closed on his foot. Rod pulled it open and shoved his way inside. One zombie, covered in blood, was almost on top of him as Henry shoved Tori inside the room. The zombie was inches from ripping off his face.

"Close the door!" he screamed. *I'm gonna die a zombie.* A long powerful arm reached out, grabbed the neck of his pursuer and jerked it from its feet. Henry watched in awe as Slam Dunk Jones tried to stuff the zombie soldier in his mouth, which seemed to open as wide as his head. Henry's brain cringed as the giant zombie bit down on the metal skull with a crunch.

Rod pulled his gaping face inside the locker, and Tori sealed the door.

"You tried to kill us!" Rod pointed at Rudy and Weege.

Rudy said, "We thought you were zombies!"

"Really? Then why did you two buttheads try to lock us out?" Rod added, his mighty chest heaving as he fought for breath.

Rudy's eyes were all over Tori, and Weege began to stammer, "There was no time—"

Whack!

Rod dropped Weege with his left.

Whack!

Tori dropped Rudy with her zombie right.

"Nice shot, Honey," Henry said.

Safe behind the glass, they witnessed the zombie fight of the century. The Rifle and Slam Dunk were pulling apart one of the zombie soldiers. It reminded Henry of two dogs fighting over a bone. Henry could hear the fabric tearing on the zombie soldier's suit as it was pulled apart. Slam Dunk pulled the helmet from the zombie and slung it into the glass, causing them to all jump back. Henry checked the lock on the door, held his chest, and slid down along the wall.

"Everyone okay?" he asked.

Rod nodded, "Everyone but these two ass-bags."

Tori curled up beside him, shivering. "What now, Henry?"

"Let's just pray help arrives before we run out of air."

"What?"

"Just kidding." He allowed himself a smile and kissed her on the head. "How's it look out there, Rod?"

"There's a zombie staring in the window."

"Really?" Henry got up and looked.

A skull-faced zombie in full zombie gear was looking right in the window. In the darkness, he swore he could see something glimmer behind its eyes. He was certain the he was being watched. It made him angry. He offered a salute. *Damn World Humanitarian Society.*

The zombie walked away, towards the door. In the background, the giants were still slugging it out with the zombie soldiers. One of the small soldiers was hoisted up and stuffed inside a nearby basketball rim.

"I wish I had my phone to catch that one!"

The outside of the door groaned. The lever was being jostled from the other side.

"It can't get in here, can it?" Tori said.

"No, it's a manual lock, like the Day Care."

Henry wasn't so sure that the zombie wouldn't figure it out.

"Can we get out?"

"These doors lock from the inside or outside. The mechanism is simple enough. We used these pins," Henry pointed to the long rod of metal dropped in the hasp in the door, "to secure them. I've used the pin on the inside. We're safe, so long as no one uses a pin on the outside. If they do that, we're stuck."

28

WASHINGTON, DC

BLOOD WAS COURSING through him like a rushing river, and the WHS security officer told him to step on the scanner. Nate's eyes flitted over to Walker, who had just passed through. The wry man had his back to him as he chatted with other WHS officers. *This isn't going to work. It's not possible.* He was running through scenarios of escape plans. What would they do if they discovered it was him? What about finger-prints? He wiped his palms on his pants as he stepped in front of the screen. What about his eyes? Did they not have records of those, too? He swallowed hard as a neon light illuminated his face. As far as he knew, he had never been fingerprinted before. No retinal scans that he knew of. But certainly the WHS had some way to keep track of him. A micro tag perhaps.

Beep.

He felt like he was about to pee himself as the outline of his skull appeared on the screen. Walker had told him to be calm. The skull-face technology was new, but effective. People could alter many things about themselves, but the entire skull wasn't likely. Hence the reconstructive surgery.

Beep.

Something was wrong. Another officer was viewing the scan on the monitor as a discrepancy was being pointed out. Nate felt like the man was poking him in the eyes as the tall man's slender finger tapped the screen. *They know it's me!*

He could see he skull matching up with another on the monitor. The name Rick Jones appeared, the same as his ID that he had scanned. So what was the problem? He cleared his throat.

"I don't have all day, gentlemen."

They ignored his comments. He could see more members of the heavily armed group move in closer. *Geez I'm dead.*

Beep.

Walker slid back over and said, "What's the hold up, boys? We have to get over to the press room stat."

With a penetrating gaze, the taller man replied, "Colonel, Officer Jones's heart rate is at 120. What happened, did you have him jog over here?"

"It wouldn't be the first time." A small laugh came from the crowd. "Since when are we monitoring heart rates?"

"Sorry, Colonel Walker, but a new regulation came out hours ago. They boost security every year. One nonsensical procedure after the other. I think they're looking for someone, but they won't say."

Walker was rubbing his chin.

"Hmmm ... so does my man check out, other than a jumpy heart rate? It is his first convention rodeo, you know."

"Everything's fine other than a runner's heart rate."

"So, what's the new procedure book say?"

The man opened up a notebook that sat on the counter and ran his finger down the pages. As he read the worst out loud Nate became mortified.

"... irregular heart rates that arouse suspicion can call for a full cavity search with proper authority."

Walker smiled wide under his mirrored glasses as he said, "Well, get the rubber gloves, I've got things to do."

"We'll try to make it quick," the man smiled, "barring any unforeseen objects found in the rectum."

Ten humiliating minutes later, Nate was following Walker through the convention center with a funny walk.

"Gee thanks, that's just what I needed. I'm all loosened up now," he fumed.

"I told you to keep your heart rate down."

"Easier said than done."

"You did fine. I didn't think we'd make it this far. As of an hour ago, our people hadn't hacked the system yet to update your profile. I was sweating bullets, but my heart rate was slow."

"Maybe that's because you don't have a heart."

"Maybe because I don't need one." Walker stopped him in the hall. "Now listen up. We're going in that room." He pointed with his finger. "I'm posting you near the front tables. Keep your hands down. Stand. Observe. Listen. They'll be right in front of you, ready to take some questions after the dinner banquet. I'll check on you. Don't act. Don't respond. If you hear anything, we can cover it after we get out of here. The walls have eyes and ears; they are watching and listening. Go in."

NO!

"Yeah, I got it."

"Let's go."

Less than a minute later, Walker posted him along the wall about thirty feet from the main table. He was one of over two dozen that secured the room. The banquet hall was huge, hosting over 1000 exquisitely dressed guests from all over the world. He remembered being a big part of all of these zombie days, loving it and hating it. He must of posed for over a thousand pictures with people from everywhere inside rooms like this. Now, he stood alone, anonymous, nervous, and free. There was something exhilarating about being nobody. Eyes glanced over and passed him like he was part of the wall. *This is kind of cool.*

Walker was on the other side of the room, seated with a handful of dignitaries, looking like a body guard. A familiar voice from the head table cut through the air in uproarious laughter.

Ben Johannes

Big, old, and bald, the man looked like a white ape with a beak for a nose. He had never liked that man or his rotting cigar-smoking breath. His dirty jokes were vile, and his demeanor was cruel. There was no way that guy could be Harry.

He watched them cut up their food, some right and others left handed. Every man had a blood steak on his plate, and the handfuls of women were eating roast chicken. They were all chatting among themselves, savoring every last bit of gluttony. Nate could picture himself up there as well. He wondered if he realized how barren he seemed. He looked into the sea of tables and wondered if anyone really cared about what these people were doing. How many of them were in on their secrets? Who financed the WHS? Maybe Harry was in the crowd.

By the time dessert was served his legs were aching, and Harry hadn't made himself known. To make matters worse he couldn't make out anything that they were saying. He never heard the word Harry once. Still, he tried to envision one of them being

Harry. He went down the line one by one. He knew them all well enough, but the name plates helped.

Julie Edgerd

Clint Raven

Edgar Crawford

Jim Dunahan

Leslie McKinley

Ben Johannes

Rachel Harriet

Edward McMinnis

Anthony Ravenloft

Sally Myers

Pamela Elswick

Missing from the group were himself and Don Baker.

Harriet. Rachel. Ben Johannes was draped over her elegant figure like a cloak. It seemed unlikely that she would be the Harry, but hers was the only name that had any kind of attachment to the name Harry. Certainly, Walker and his crew had made that connection and looked into it. *This is pointless.* He wanted to leave. Start a new life. Go to Vegas and disappear. But there was another zombie apocalypse on the horizon. He didn't want anyone on Earth to go through that again.

"Anything?"

Nate's heart jumped.

"Just nod."

He shook his head a little.

Walker slapped him on the shoulder and said, "Hang in there. It's almost over, but we have to stick around until they leave."

Nate was daydreaming now; trying to take his mind off the pain in his aching legs and feet. He couldn't remember standing so long before, and he would kill a man just to be able to take a seat. At the end of the head table he overheard bits and pieces of Anthony Ravenloft's jovial conversation on his phone. The man had raven black hair, a stout build, and a row of teeth that seemed to be a mile wide. Nate had never talked to that man much. He seemed to keep to himself more so than the others. He excused himself from the table and walked closer to the wall, eyeing the audience and waving at some acquaintances. More uproarious laughter burst from Ben Johannes' throat, which caught his attention and turned Rachel Harriet's cheeks the bright color of roses. *What a pompous jerk.* It seemed like most of the room was laughing at something or another at the time, when his ears picked up something that sent a sliver of ice down his spine.

"... Take it easy, Son. I'm just pulling your leg," Anthony Ravenloft had said. Harry had said that same phrase to him over the years at least a few dozen times.

29

EPILOGUE

WASHINGTON, DC

"DON'T TAKE it so bad, Jack. It's only money."

If Don's nephew heard him, he couldn't tell. The young man smashed his computer on the park bench and screamed. The pigeons scattered into the air, leaving Don alone to bask in the moon of the chill night air. He fought the tears and the laughter as the car door slammed shut behind him. Don was getting too old for this. He needed to retire, but for a man in his position, retirement meant death.

The men and women in the West Virginia complex would be safe, for now. Henry Bawkula had proven to be a formidable man. A survivor. A threat to the WHS. Don wanted to be there when the WHS had to explain what had gone wrong. The clean up would be quick and the interrogations ugly, but they would live ... gag order pending.

He took his final swallow of coffee and closed his eyes in a moment of thanks. He was all too happy to close his computer and try to forget the tortuous scenes. *Is this what they have in store for me one day?* His inner core shuddered at the thought. He took another minute to bask in his hollow victory. Maybe he should head over to the Zombie Convention. He needed to pick some brains. The fact that he'd been told it was okay to miss this one seemed awfully strange now. He sighed, picked up his Thermos, and tried to think of some comforting words to say to Jack as he headed for the car.

Oliver sat inside as the engine warmed on the big black Cadillac. His bodyguard started to get out of his car, but Don said, "It's okay, Oliver, I can open my own door."

As he sat down in his seat, he noticed Jack was slumped over, unmoving. Adrenaline surged through him as he heard the sounds of his door locking.

"Oliver, what is this?" he stammered as he lifted his nephew's head back and noticed the bloody bullet hole in his chest.

The barrel of a silencer was pointing in his face in reply. Oliver's voice was ice cold.

"Your nephew had become quite the evil bastard, Don. He had to die."

Don shrunk back in his seat and said, "Why, Oliver? Why?"

"I told you why."

"Are you going to kill me, too?" he stammered.

"Don't you think you deserve to die after being behind the deaths of millions of people?"

"I suppose."

"Then we both agree."

BLAM!

Don felt his breathing thin as all of his strength left his body, and he fell over by his nephew's side. He could hear a song on the radio playing, and Oliver singing. He wondered if he was dead or alive.

"Don't worry, Don, you aren't going to die. But you are going to pay for what you did."

DON'T FORGET to leave a review, they are a HUGE help! LINK!

It is not over! Zombie Warfare - Book 3! Don't miss out! BUY NOW LINK!

ABOUT THE AUTHOR

Check me out on Bookbub and follow: Craig Halloran

I'd love it if you would subscribe to my newsletter and download my free books: www. craighalloran.com/email

On Facebook, you can find me at The Darkslayer Report by Craig Halloran.

Twitter, Twitter, Twitter. I am there, too: www. twitter.com/CraigHalloran

And of course, you can always email me anytime at craig@thedarkslayer.com

CRAIG'S COMPLETE BOOK LIST

OVER 100 TITLES! PURE ADRENALINE!

5 MILLION WORDS IN PUBLICATION!

EPIC FANTASY, SWORD AND SORCERY URBAN
FANTASY, SCI-FI, POST-APOC! LINKS BELOW!

FREE BOOKS

The Darkslayer: Brutal Beginnings

Nath Dragon – Quest for the Thunderstone

The Henchmen Chronicles Intro

Dragon Wars Prequel

The Odyssey of Nath Dragon Series (Prequel to Chronicles of Dragon)

Exiled: Book 1 of 5

The Odyssey of Nath Dragon Boxset (Best Deal)

The Chronicles of Dragon Series 1 (10 Books)

The Hero, the Sword and the Dragons (Book 1)

Boxset 1-5

Boxset 6-10

Collector's Edition 1-10 (Best Deal)

Tail of the Dragon, The Chronicles of Dragon, Series 2 (10 book series)

Tail of the Dragon Book #1

Boxset 1-5

Boxset 6-10

Collector's Edition 1-10 (Best Deal)

The Darkslayer Series 1 – 6 books

Wrath of the Royals (Book 1)

Boxset 1-3

Boxset 4-6

Omnibus 1-6 (Best Deal)

The Darkslayer: Bish and Bone, Series 2 (10 Book series)

Bish and Bone (Book 1 of 10)

Boxset 1-5

Boxset 6-10

Bish and Bone Omnibus (Books 1-10) (Best Deal)

Dragon Wars: 20-Book Series

Blood Brothers: Book 1 of 20

Boxset 1-5

Boxset 6-10

Boxset 11-15

Boxset 16-20

CLASH OF HEROES: Nath Dragon meets The Darkslayer

Book 1 of 3

Special Edition - Books 1-3 (Best Deal)

The Supernatural Bounty Hunter Files (10 book series)

Smoke Rising: Book 1 of 10

Boxset 1-5

Boxset 6-10

Collector's Edition 1-10 (Best Deal)

The Henchmen Chronicles 5-Book Series

The King's Henchmen - Book 1 of 5

The Henchmen Chronicles Collection: Books 1-5

Zombie Impact Series

Zombie Day Care: Book 1

Zombie Rehab: Book 2

Zombie Warfare: Book 3

Boxset: Books 1-3 (Best Deal)

The Gamma Earth Cycle

Escape from the Dominion

Flight from the Dominion

Prison of the Dominion

The Sorcerer's Power Series

The Sorcerer's Curse: Book 1 of 5

The Red Citadel and the Sorcerer's Power (All 5 Books)

The Misadventures of Dan - Drama/Comedy

Gorgon Thunder-Bot Incinerator of Worlds (1 book, childrens)